THE PAWNE[...]
Anthony Au[sgang]

AUSGANG
SURREAL POPULIST
AUSGANGART.COM

2013

EXIT
PUBLISHING

2013

FIRST EDITION MARCH 2013

Library of Congress Cataloging-in-Publication Data
Anthony Ausgang, 1959-
THE PAWNEE REPUBLICAN / Anthony Ausgang
ISBN 978-1-4839829-3-9
1. Deconstruction in the Random-Word Age — Meditations on. I Title

Anthony Ausgang
811 Micheltorena
Los Angeles, CA 90026
www.ausgangart.com

Manufactured in the United States of America

THE PAWNEE REPUBLICAN

OR...

A SKIRT CHASER IN SLACKTOWN

FIRST EDITION 2013

ART DIRECTION & COVER DESIGN: ANDY TAKAKJIAN
BOOK LAYOUT: PORTAL DESIGN
COVER PAINTING: ANTHONY AUSGANG

EXIT PUBLISHING

YELP REVIEWS OF THE PAWNEE REPUBLICAN

"I am always on a budget and I was very happy with my experience. *The Pawnee Republican* is extremely interesting and the chapters are just the right size."

"We stayed for a week and read *The Pawnee Republican* in an old room where I think someone was murdered. The plot is OK but there were beer cans and cigarette butts everywhere."

"The three best things about this book are absolutely the set up, the conflict, and the resolution. If you're thinking of reading something suuuuuuper cheap you should probably just drop the extra couple bucks and read *The Pawnee Republican*."

"All in all, a great book! I highly recommend *The Pawnee Republican* if you need to get over the inevitable discomfort of eating too much meat."

"*The Pawnee Republican* was absolutely nothing spectacular, I mean, I'm not complaining it was fine I guess. Its kinda like hey I got what I paid for."

"There are some books you read and you say that was a great story, but there are others where you throw your copy on the table, admitting genius. *The Pawnee Republican* is that kind of book; its not just a read, its an awesome experience!"

CONTENTS

FOREWORD

by Shana Nys Dambrot

"So, WTF, he would craft his reply partly as a joke, a bit of filthy farce rent to its very twain by fiction."

Anthony Ausgang loves to turn a phrase. He fairly lives for a quality pun, and that has been as true in his decades of painting as it has become in his budding career as a novelist. His paintings themselves have something of the character of literary comedy, hilarious without being either stupid or slapstick, too well crafted to be simple one-liners, yet too smart and cheeky to be taken altogether seriously. Ausgang's visual art manipulates elements of high-minded optical theory, using an impressive array of permutations on hard-edge abstraction, supersaturated palettes, and intensive patterns juxtaposed in elaborate and eye-grabbing arrangements, to which he then adds cartoon cats. Why cats? In typical Ausgang fashion, it is mostly because he needed an image/object to lend both a functional narrative clue and compositional aspects of space and scale to what would otherwise be complete abstraction -- but it's also because, as any glancing perusal of the internet will demonstrate, "everyone loves pictures of cats." Occasionally, instead of cartoon cats he adds hyper-stylized hot-rods, for all the same reasons.

"After all, the strength of art lies in being simple, nude, and poor."

Because of this uniquely personal but also broadly zeitgeisty approach merging art-historical studio-painting concerns with iconography culled from popular culture, his paintings have become stars in the Pop Surrealism firmament -- but that is, of course, not really the whole story. In a way, his turn to the written word represents much less of a break in his artistic activity than would a change in painting style. That's because, in a very real sense, he has managed the neat trick of transferring the clear core of his creative process from the easel to the keyboard in a way that sheds light on both. Addressing underlying issues of how we have trained ourselves to structure and consume information for maximum efficiency rather than the inconvenient specifics of actual experience, in both his paintings and his prose, it's the underlying framework that is really what's under scrutiny. Swapping cats and racecars for spam email and random word generators, he attempts to graft familiar nonsense onto abstract poetics and come up with something impossible that still follows the laws of perception. If the paintings are Pop Surrealism, then maybe the novels could be called Post-Structuralist Surrealism.

"Blue cigarette smoke curled above the dome of his head like a staircase that nobody may go up or down."

The theory of Post-Structuralism, which was in full currency in the early decades of the 20th Century, and was closely followed by the related school of Deconstructivism, existed in opposition to the rules of literature and language, seeking in a way to strip language down to such a state of laid-bare syntactical armature so as to allow for a right proper examination of its most basic immutable constitution, eschewing assumptions and semiotic shortcuts. In Gertrude Stein's archetypally Post-Structuralist sentence, "A rose is a rose is a rose," unassailable fact and utter nonsense coexist in a state of extreme specificity in which metaphor is self-reflexive and the pre-existing archive of the collective unconscious fills in the rest. Highlighting the malleability and contrarian nature of signs and symbols and the arbitrary vagaries of language, what Ausgang calls "the internet's broad immaterial twilight" is Post-Structuralist heaven.

> "He stood with his eyes closed, imagining the color black apart from its visual appearance."

The Pawnee Republican stakes out a fairly conventional plot structure, focusing on a singular, centralized storyline. It's a story of jealousy and revenge, intimacy, comeuppance, and karma -- an old-fashioned morality play, or, if you prefer, an immorality play. Paring down the plot more effectively sets off the flourishes of the prose, making it easier for the casual reader to relax into the baroque ebb and flow of the spun-sugar language itself, in which most of the salient action unfolds inside elaborate similes. Descriptive action, protagonistic introspection, and motivational insight are expressed through poetical equivalencies rather than documentarian accounts. The plot gets out of its own way so that its subversive, gorgeous form can stay the star. In other words, there's just enough cartoon cat to keep you grounded amid the expanse of giddy abstraction.

"For artists do not make their gods, they only create situations from which god must save them."

For example, by turning off their spam filters.

—Shana Nys Dambrot
Los Angeles, March 2013

MODUS OPERANDI

by Anthony Ausgang

I'm probably the only person that not only reads their SPAM emails, but also saves them to examine again later. For me, each day brings a fascinating cascade of tainted e-pistles guaranteeing million dollar deposits to my bank account and/or extra inches to my penis. I just can't resist opening an email from a med company in Canada that discreetly promises to help me "avoid outworn sleeping pins in any poignant lace situation" or a Nigerian who politely assures me I'll "never again have to worry about a collection agency's combustible retinal bootstrappers" because I just won two million dollars.

After years of saving these emails in one huge word document I found that the morass of words read like an abstract novel, and just for the hell of it I decided to reign in the chaos by replacing some pronouns with names culled from the flood of verbiage. This unifying element unexpectedly created the roots of strange and abstract plot, and with a great deal of editing and help from online random word generators, a book began to take shape.

In order to continue skirting the brink of incomprehensibility but make the narrative lucid, it was necessary to periodically insert logical sentences. Ultimately I decided that not every sentence in the book had to be constructed with SPAM blurts or random text, but each paragraph did have to contain as many fragments as possible lifted from them. This method took the plot development out of my exclusive control, and I was constantly frustrated by not being able to find text that suited the direction I wanted the action to take; at times I only had as much of an idea as a first time reader about what was going to occur in this book.

THE
PAWNEE
REPUBLICAN

OR...

A SKIRT CHASER IN SLACKTOWN

A MEASURED PRAYER

A **huge racing car flashed through the avenues** of Hill Town Eye, covered with dust and broadcasting all the indications of having come a great distance at a fair speed. Within its compartment Puss Titter leaned forward in her seat and clutched the arm of her companion, Dude Noway. They had just emerged from the country lane that passes the bubble farms and were now pulsing along the broad highroad lined with heaps of trifles, finally grinding to a stop in front of a maternal apartment building. Puss Titter radiated across the desert of the sidewalk and entered her loose refuge as the artillery sound of the departing engine faded.

The Necrotatorium Apartments sank within its network of ruins, biting at the afternoon's lure like a measured prayer. The building was made of a clumsy mosaic material, appearing as if it had been subjected to the worldly dissatisfactions of a moribund imagination. It had once been a happy home where love signs rarely ceased and Nature's grand law of order had there reigned with exactness sure. Now it was as if the wings of time were not able to glide through an atmosphere so impure. In the windows no joy-lit life appeared, for the budding blossoms of poignant times passed by the lost residence no less now than all the decades before.

The building rose from the murk of the urban provinces like a perch fitted with all the archaic conveniences of a meltdown life. Puss Titter closed the door of her apartment, her contempt for the world backing up the discreet withdrawl. She sat by the window in her impossible appearance, looking through her telescope at the close shaves being celebrated on the broad avenues:

Perambulating the pavement like the best troops in Mexico entering Texas were the MILFs Ms. Like Awesome and Cherry Draws Beat, the crowd in front of The Nasty Castle parting for them like personnel trained to handle ruminant animals. Dude Noway had stopped and now stood at the outside automatic teller machine of The Bank of Hill Town Eye, rapturously repeating the amount of his paycheck to himself. In a drum circle at the park, the Algonquian chief Falling Bong Water leaped from the inner circle to dance alone between the drummers, like a prospector who has taken his planks and gone to seek a fortune elsewhere. Through the means of peyote he was said to possess a degree of familiarity with the Almighty beyond that of the most devoted sacristan, not unlike a German peasant wont to address the sun and the moon familiarly.

The Annual Parade of The Sleeping Elitists advanced through the streets, this year's somnolent Caesars dreaming of dollars and women from their pallets.

Puss Titter relished the consequence of Hill Town Eye's gathering picture, her countenance overrun with the murmurs of admiration and envy she imagined circulating around the room, as if courtiers of the great hall of Hymbercourt had been stimulated by her worthy sunshine. Indeed, her day with Dude Noway had reminded Puss Titter that there are few moments in life that provide a manna as fine and trouble free as post-coital bliss.

Dude Noway was a Wrath Radio DJ specializing in the finest Choral Metal pulsing on the prescription airwaves. He broadcast Satan's music as if calling his master, the worthy darkness delighting his fans like a moonwalk in the sky. Each night Dude Noway would pull some degraded stunt, his punch raving against the jungle as the tunes beamed into the ruins; with his style and smirk he could have led God on a VIP tour of Hell.

It was over the engrossing assurances of such a smile that Puss Titter and Dude Noway met, both basking in the glow of their unlimited cordiality as they took mental notes of the scene for any future rights of petition.

Puss Titter's postponed brain had reacted like an optical lawnmower and there was no false delight in her smiling warrant for his attentions; she felt as ripe as a burst fruit. Dude Noway dipped his shoulders beneath his smile and moved in as though he were a damaged neighbor, making no discretion about openly reading her breasts. He then leaned back in his royal leisure with a smiling confidence, like some variant acquaintance marching into a haircut. Dude Noway seemed mean, manipulative and merciless, just the sort of dangerous man on which Puss Titter feasted. But he delivered something more formidable than her appetite could handle; even with all his Native American stoicism, Dude Noway nourished a smiling confidence that no one could have assumed with better grace.

Puss Titter had never heard of such a subject before and from that point forward would ride night and day to fall back upon his pillow and enjoy the cordial reception. Theirs was a classic romance, full of orderly little secrets and deep breaths of satisfaction in meadows still green amidst unscathed groves of flowering trees.

But there is a time limit to such psychic prosperity, and Puss Titter had recently returned to the world she shared with mud and luggage.

Lately, Dude Noway had been acting like some jaded philosopher lost in an unanswerable forest: it was as if another purpose had blurred his aim. She feared that the love in Dude Noway's eyes was giving way to the agitation found in a priest who has lost the devotion of his tailored flock. Perhaps her current existence affronted invitation from any of the lively packages that may have been thought natural in the advances of Dude Noway, but that seemed unlikely. Something had to be done, and like an incomplete recipe, she had to refine a strategy.

Puss Titter knew that sweetness of behavior is often considered a sign of weakness, so she decided to test Dude Noway's affections by sending him temptation in the form of a virtual harlot from the internet's broad immaterial twilight. This E-whore would put great energy of purpose in the pursuit of Dude Noway, inviting him to experience phenomenal sex whenever and wherever he craved it.

Dude Noway would expose his true self, either proving himself as an unfaithful lover or the best and brightest of his generation.

Like the work of all great inventors, Puss Titter's propulsive scheme might be misunderstood, but she was sure it would cause their love to again grow like the grass and rose leaves of a garden. Still, before this conclusion could be formulated and expressed, she had to take into account that this was not an actual fact but rather some kind of still as yet unknown. The scheme could backfire and Puss Titter would become Dude Noway's prisoner of war, suffering from the impure motivation of such an unwholesome surprise.

In the stormy sky over Hill Town Eye two wrens swept high above the feverish hordes, their shapes abstracting in the cosmic drift. Watching the pathetic film in the streets below, Puss Titter felt a combination of the tranquility that comes from an anchor holding firm and the absolute consolation of living in the present. The moments rolled on with the discontented whine of a deflected shot, once again reminding Puss Titter that the most important fact appearing in things which live for only the next second cannot be hurt, it can only effect their rescue.

THE YOKE OF HYPOSARCIDES

Although she lived on the campus of The University of Whatever, Professor Cherry Draws Beat was unable to connect with her students since most of them partied like unwound lions on a merry ship. It made more sense for Cherry Draws Beat to broadcast her lessons to only such castaways of the noisome vessels as seemed interested. After all, the majority preferred to see the facts she espoused lying at the bottom of the ocean, not in unnavigable volumes of history.

Such is the fateful preparation of circumstance.

Then, one day as she took breakfast in her garden, serenaded by the mystic luxury and ecstatic mirth of birdsong, Cherry Draws Beat made an epic mistake. She opened a spam email, just another lying exposé in beaten prose, and the Yoke of Hyposarcides virus caulked up her computer, causing the complete cessation of all its functions. That in itself was not unusual; the disturbing variance was that for some freak substantific reason Cherry Draws Beat also contracted the virus, and this sempiternal curse left her unable to read or write emails on any device. It was as though she was making ready to be lost, and there wasn't any unsavoury cure she could take to do something about it.

As a violent consequence of this medical condition Cherry Draws Beat was forced to hire an employee who would read and write her emails for her, and to this end she would depend on her wits.

Knowing that although intellect on the surface is called reason, its mass is thinly clothed in the deciduous undergrowth of instinct. Now it was no nay that thitherward she turned and went wisely, removing the folly from her head and crushing it like a catapult as she moved past the brigantines of false promise.

******

Cherry Draws Beat found the imported Americans strange, they would cross town for praise of little value but spend the dinner hour in the street, lazing in their faulty posture with a dry fury as if forbidding midnight to occur. It seemed only right to spurn such imports and hire an indigenous native, one raised in a clean conjugal forest hamlet built on sacred grounds. She would make it a point to find a tribesman of principles, one whose freedom of will could not be sullied by any anecdotal divinity.

Out in the streets Cherry Draws Beat ignored the chimneys doing penance in the plosive storm of their cajoling vapors. Avoiding the avowed and hypocritical enemies of incarnate love, she progressed in her splendid pageantry through myriads of dimly lit arcades and clumsy parking lots. She disregarded Grub Walk, which passed The Opprobrium Lounge, where the contrary flesh of the longskirted death wenches roiled in drunken fervor. The women made dismal howlings, as if to bind up their wounds, and she imagined, with more than a common curiosity, if she shared a creator with such wretches. The crowd filled Cherry Draws Beat with an inordinate longing for the sight of blood but she compromised by greeting the transmuted wives out front as she passed. More poached dames and their wilted gapes lined the boulevards, their exhausted fire forcing Cherry Draws Beat toward The Faecal Breech Café with an authoritative unfriendliness.

Waves of platonic care washed over her chiseled features as she confirmed her steps into the chamber, and no one seemed to notice Cherry Draws Beat as she creased through the interior's ecology. It was as if Montessori's didactic approach had deadened their senses and an infinite symbol had taken control of their eyesight. Crews of structural citizens mumbled under clouds of tobacco smoke, scratching at the peripheral attributes of their unfinished breakdowns. As they sat to their meals of filth, they seemed like breathing heaps, speaking of the wonders that love brings, and nursing wild projects that had never entered their heads. The Fraudulent Kid And His Dispiriting Mandate played irritating nostalgia rock as two famous barristers sat by the corner of the stage, discussing illegal downloads. Near them a matrix volunteer texted with his phone as the empty hours yawned before him like the frozen laugh of a sore vegetarian. There seemed to be no candidates for Cherry Draws Beat's employment so, with a backward flip, she punted her sensitive worries toward the door.

Then the tavern's appearance froze like high res porn on a shitty computer; she had spied her Algonquian friend Falling Bong Water sitting at the bar, elucidating his well-rehearsed miseries to a woman apparently convinced of his cordial affections.

Cherry Draws Beat approached the sachem and explained that she needed to hire an adjutant ASAP since her emails were queuing up like an overgrown psalmody.

Falling Bong Water listened to Cherry Draws Beat's appeal since they shared the same pleasure of joy and love for the sake of wisdom, but the chief was eager to return to his philandering. The private lives of industrious people and their articulate declarations could not hold his interest for long. So, claiming his instrument to be infallible, Falling Bong Water told Cherry Draws Beat to visit Pacificatory Beach the following night. There, like a frayed lion stalking jolly cows, she would meet The Pawnee Republican, a personage able to meet the requirements of her need.

With this answer Falling Bong Water turned away as if ambition had led him in that direction, choosing to neither disown the imputation nor acknowledge its truth. It seemed that there were other forces of modification at work, like an epidemic that has recently swept through a country, leaving memorials at whose curious epitaphs and quaint phrases one can either scoff or marvel.

Each of us may have a wish to try something new, but still cannot walk alone in the forest at night without trembling. As Cherry Draws Beat trekked back to her crib through the swineherds, loiterers and alamode sultanas, she felt like a brave woman wasted in the winter retreat of an emperor's army.

A NEEDLESS SURPRISE

Puss Titter sat at a computer, her intentions oiling the cool choice she had just made like a government industry. Dude Noway would soon be receiving an email delivering the unexpected and boisterous joy that comes from the sexual interest of strangers. She expected that this abstract would initiate a string of events ultimately proving Dude Noway's allegiance to her firm anatomy, but she was equally prepared for infidelity's unpleasantness.

After all, her unreserved projection needed no introduction, and any observer whose eyes were absorbed by such attention would be sadly puzzled.

The e-vitation was a collage of spam emails that Puss Titter had recently received; she had felt that anything less proven would fail to send Dude Noway on the routed quest. No pornographic eloquence was too great if the tactic got Dude Noway to cross enough territory to reach what he supposed as heaven, but she knew that even with such lust her emails could be ignored. Still, Puss Titter was sure that the girth of such an accomplishment would only tempt his submission nearer.

Ultimately the letter was a false courier, sent to mouth the higher proofs of a narrative normally ignored, like an immigrant articulating an irregular conjugation.

The Bots sped the email along, bundling up the bits and bytes with a tactical grace as the cybernetic transmission engines instantaneously delivered their information to Dude Noway's inbox. But its forward progress was thwarted there by inertia of its addressee, crashed out as usual with his meerschaum of chronic spilled on his shirt like a shaft of emerald light across the land. At that moment the rapid stream of his life showed hardly a ripple, and any reasonable native would have condoned the use of fireworks to inaugurate Dude Noway's return to consciousness.

But soon he awoke of his own volition, like a needless surprise that has decided to express itself. Indulging the most necessary ingredient of his existence, Dude Noway immediately checked the perpetual megabytes of his email, fearing that in his stupor he had missed an e-vite to some rare event that cannot occur twice. Instead he found the usual attendant nonsense of annoying confidences and political noise clogging up his mailbox, the superficial synonyms foaming past him like cars on an amazed freeway. He was censoring the backlogged overflow of gratuitous contacts when his intolerance was suddenly arrested by a compelling idiom in the subject line of an urgent e-pigram:

From: Oriflamme Plowjobber
To: Dude Noway
Subject: Blazing Flesh!
Reply-To: Oriflamme@straponfiesta.com

Hey Dude! Do you always be delirious of an attractive lady? Well name the job you want for your cock coz I am your new essential strapon domme riding in from the road to trouble! Your cheeks will daub rife as each cunningly sexy stroke of my burdensome rubber dick adds a sizable boost to your butt cheeks, making you scream dog-ear for forgiveness! And later, if you're lucky, we can watch hot hardcore strapon gender videos together as my noticeably protrusive cane flogs your champion!
Can you picture such an elegant addition to your minority inches of dick? I thought you might!
I live with you in the same place or close to it and I've always wanted to get to meet a man nearby for this intense discreet fun. Tell me about you, what are you into, what turns you on etc etc? I love to be the central slut, dominating my mannish slave with all my thrusting attention-grabbers, do you be fond of it too?
We can do whatever you want; I'm ready for it!
You got anything fun planned for the week? I haven't yet; I could do with some fun LOL! Let me know if you have some extra time and if you're interested we can set something up. XOXOXO

Thanks for joining the Great Cocks Crusade!
Oriflamme Plowjobber

Dude Noway was well acquainted with female charlatanism but he found the perversion of this curious suitor intriguing, which made him feel obliged to respond with proper expressions that would bewitch her who had bewitched him. Even though he was pretty sure that his suitor was an as yet unknown longskirted Spamming Bot, he still believed in good fortune, and it was possible some actual woman had sent the dalliance.

So, WTF, he would craft his reply partly as a joke, a bit of filthy farce rent to its very twain by fiction.

After a bong hit, Dude Noway's inhibition melted away like wastebutter and he began his response in kind to the spirit that had touch of this Oriflamme Plowjobber. Being in no haste, Indian fashion, he hunted and pecked, letting his budget-speak seduce this impish goddess, and his reply was full of direct urgings to vivacious service. He drew closer to his computer and jabbed at the interlarded declarations, the words struggling to their correct positions. Finally, he finished the letter and hit send, feeling much like a successful high-income author writing the last sentence of a novel.

Being young, such lightness of mind was a joyous companion to Dude Noway, but he knew his noblespirited words could lead to insatiable misunderstandings and he would have to take great care. Puss Titter's constant womenchurching of his doings provided little room for error in his game and he would have to watch for her ambuscades to his front and flanks.

It was obvious that without adequate masquerade the whole affair would fail with the crash of broken crockery in a collapsed home.

Dude Noway had done nothing yet, but he already felt as if he were a man accusing himself before a tribunal. He did not consider his flirting with Oriflamme Plowjobber to be a problem; it was the stress of the required secrecy that threatened Dude Noway like a mutinous spearman standing in the ranks behind him. After all, Puss Titter had done nothing to deserve the striking of this immoral chord in her blended canticle. None of her finer qualities were substantially the same as those incident to ownership; obviously it was he, Dude Noway, who possessed the vulgar heart.

THE PAWNEE REPUBLICAN

A bugle call was heard all the way across the seas, summoning Cherry Draws Beat to lift her eyes and make a note of every detail in the beach spread out before her. Normally she would be tripping around the industrial sector, chilled by death and the application of fear that recurs so often in the mind. She felt like a imprisoned woman being questioned while the crime of which she is accused still unfolds. It was measured work, this lingering around for someone she had never met, and Cherry Draws Beat hoped to graduate soon from the incident.

Perhaps this barbarous business was a man's mission after all, and that was the only way the truth would emerge.

Across the strand a man got out of an authoritative motorcar, his appearance spraying across the beachscape like bullets. He resembled a heathen inhabitant of Palestine, as if carried forth from the corruption of medieval make-believe. As he gazed on the wide expanse of ocean he appeared to be feasting on something rich and novel that is not brought before ordinary men. He reeked of unpleasant and peculiar joys, creating an inquietude sufficient enough to require increased precaution in all he encountered. The stranger seemed to leave his mysteries yet to be revealed, like an ill-advised excavation.

Blue cigarette smoke curled above the dome of his head like a staircase that nobody may go up or down.

Cherry Draws Beat approached through the various objects under obstruction, aware of the sensations her appearance called forth. But somehow she knew, even before her rhetoric's deadline had passed, that the unbalanced guest before her was The Pawnee Republican. Still, her train of thought, to which necessity gave birth, continued to fill her with apprehensions.

Thanks to a feature of perspective, the stranger became considerably larger as Cherry Draws Beat advanced.

After their introductions the pair strode to a nearby grogshop, the silence of the murdered city surrounding them as a billion blades of grass danced in time with the wind. Nothing was to be heard other than the heavy tread of passing robots on the stone pavement, like wanderers returning to their normal space on earth's vast level.

The companions soon reached the Holy Farces District, where by decree there could not be a single temple wherein to worship God. Here the senses of both men and women were to be indulged in one way or another, maximizing those unjust liberties that are the bulwarks of scandalizing pleasure. Too many methods of imposing heathen excess upon moral restriction were available, and even youngsters that had stepped out so jauntily at first were soon footsore and dazed from the Olympian corruption. Groups of heretical partisans and depraved addicts marauded through the streets, encouraging the gonorrhoea of disordered lechery like noisome goblins released from a dungeon.

Comfort and happiness were achieved only through decadence, as if that alone was sufficient to satisfy those needs.

The pair entered The Satyr's Sojourn, a dying landmark that looked like countless satisfactions had been denied to all attendants of its tilted decay. It functioned as a cradle for the crabbed dotage of the unfit philosophers that made up its clientele, no well paid or polished praegustator twice dared refreshment in its tattered abyss. It had become a blood trap for the frayed gods whose noble spirited munificence had run dry, the rhythmical cadence of their light feet replaced with a lumbering apathy. Soon Cherry Draws Beat had freshened her calculating powers with enough drink that she was able see clearly in the ultra-violet portion of the lamplight. As she explained herself to The Pawnee Republican he leaned sloppily landwards on his tuffet, the cognitive palaver of their frump and arbitration budging him with its impenetrable momentum. Perspiration flowed from his head, making it appear as if he had been botched up out of dregs and relics by ignoble hands in a hurried manner. He looked like some vague figure described in sign language.

A little sandy cat crept across the floor as if exploring the wreckage of kingdoms.

The Indian had a high sense of personal honor that counterbalanced any of his own misgivings about the enterprise. This had not always been the case, he had only recently started refusing illegal activities that would lower his mind and debase his heart. Although he still felt closer to illicit affairs than any lawful business, he was now making attempts to distinguish order from disorder and harmony from discord. Perhaps when he had explored this fresh approach a little more he would not be left clinging to such productions of mother nature as were at hand, but dwelling righteously in a reality of his own design.

The Pawnee Republican began to loosen up, turning the gloomy and perilous scene into one that was polished bright with acid and friction, like the brass casings of ammunition.

Cherry Draws Beat offered the wages like some topical mathematician reading aloud from an algebraic journal, adding half a bushel of seed corn and some tobacco as a gesture of goodwill. She spoke in a voice as smooth as silver, the vacuum of space around her shimmering as though she was forming a necessary appendage to a history of the Conquest. Still, Cherry Draws Beat's revelations were entirely different from any light that could darken her counsel with God.

It was entirely something else, these difficult questions whose foregone conclusions were not yet formulated. She drew a deep breath and made a mental note to find an appropriate word to express her meaning.

Apparently The Pawnee Republican saw no advantage to making an outcry; perhaps he was simply hiding himself from the tyranny of abstractions that could testify against him. As there seemed to be no debate, he accepted the pay and agreed to start in the morning.

Finding themselves no longer being questioned, they rose from the table like lees in a shaken bottle of spirits that is borne to the bridal stateroom of a huge steamer.

The two left The Satyr's Sojourn as if climbing from a natural cave in the rock, the abrupt opening on to the earth seeming like a hole rent in reality. They soon parted company in the roasted declarations of the streetlamps, escaping like rabbits that could not have disappeared more quickly.

MS. LIKE AWESOME

Inside of The Boy Meats Grill, the snotty method authors served up their anguished prose like codpiece chitterlings in a horrid soup. To Puss Titter it was as if a beggar's ill favored and hazardous fart had interrupted the speech of a devout soul, the very air soiled by the scampering discharge. She spied Ms. Like Awesome, Hilltown Eye's most eligible MILF, sitting at the bar listening to the cadence of some drunk's smutty accolade while curling away in defensive revulsion from the drooping passion of his blubber lip. Puss Titter elbowed her way through the puny physiognomy and sat next to the pair, in terrupting their alcoholic declensions with no apology.

Within minutes the infernal suitor departed, leaving behind his tip and a scrap of paper with the MILF's phone number, apparently preferring the bedlam of the raucous crowd to the false conviviality of an interloping drinkspiller.

As she scooped the change and chit into her purse, Puss Titter launched into the tufts of her plan to ensnare Dude Noway, trying to convince Ms. Like Awesome to play the part of Oriflamme Plowjobber. The windows jarred with the cannonade of her request but the MILF seemed unconvinced, as if she had been led, by wrong reports, to believe that something of this nature could only result in a tempest of trouble for her soul. Still, Ms. Like Awesome was intrigued; after all, the opportunity to play a slut at another woman's request was disconcertingly attractive. For a time she lingered in doubt, as if somewhere there was a written version of Puss Titter's appeal that differed, but finally Ms. Like Awesome stepped over to that region where common curiosity is the best motivator, and she declared her agreement to the scheme.

The women decided to celebrate the sacred ingenuity of their bold alignment by drinking until they were unfit to stand and had to be propped upright.

Around them the blame attendants and inconsiderate faggots worked their dialects as if they were virginal wolves coughing in some conjugal monastery. In the crowd of disagreeable sensations Puss Titter had never appeared so charming, like a young lady dowered with gold and good looks. She wafted through the bar's vacuum, celestial and thievish, secure in the queendom of her sensational intention to bring Dude Noway to the brink. Ms. Like Awesome followed in her sharpened lechery, mentally exercising the invention of their lawful conspiracy.

The pair vigorously attacked their drinks with brutal, substantial thrusts. They were fraud stars, their bunco rousing the sleepers that surrounded them like judgment claps. The pair drank freely, ignoring the annoyed comminations of the spurned males that had filled their cups.

After all, the strength of art lies in being simple, nude, and poor.

It seemed that The Faecal Breech was proceeding to an inordinately long and weary orgasm that would bring the premeditated partying of the natives to a lingering conclusion. Still, even the best natures need to be reminded that perseverance and failure are often foreseen in the great plan of their weakness, as Puss Titter was about to find out.

A Southern Governor stood in the corner, his little finger thicker than his loins.

Across the congregation of pompadours and vigorous extremities, Puss Titter spied a man whose volcanic features shed innocence like a soul called out from its tomb for no use. His immutable and irresistible stance declared him absolute master, yet in reality he commanded only part of the ground upon which he stood. Nevertheless, all represent one and the same, and far from showing any deep regret for his crime of discarded virtue, he talked animatedly with his entourage of heathens.

It was The Pawnee Republican, tearing down his not-yet-spoken-of-past and gliding along as he boldly exposed the thoughts at the bottom of his mind.

Puss Titter blasted off into the crowd, holding the ordinances of the Lord blameless as she made her way in the direction of this man whose appearance and appointments filled her with a lustful bravado. She was sure that the endless joys she lacked would finally be delivered to her shielding hands if she could just spend one night in the brazen-cleft pavilion of the stranger's bedchamber. As Puss Titter neared him, her faith in love returned with the earnestness of a call to arms that is raised at daybreak, and all thoughts of Dude Noway vanished as the interloper blinded her senses, pulling the breath out of her body with the heretical vociferousness of parrots biting at a nest.

At last Puss Titter extended her hand to The Pawnee Republican, who grasped it as if he were a climber holding on to the edge of a ravine. Yet he seemed specifically distinct from the notion of contact, the rest of his physique as still as the stones of an ancient tower. But blood moves as one calls it to mind, and when Puss Titter convulsively clasped The Pawnee Republican's hand they pulled together like shirkers forced by public opinion into exerting themselves. Up close he seemed neither tall nor short, with the wicked and dangerous edge of a cleaving iceberg that has been stirred over a hot fire until smooth. There was a light shooting from his dark eyes so deeply set in the black lines of his gray visage, and it carried Puss Titter beyond human capability until she felt a faintness in the asylum of her body as though she had taken ether or an anaesthetic before an operation.

The Pawnee Republican had perfectly administered his system of psychic forgery and Puss Titter followed him to a narrow exit that opened on the alley, leaving the long drawn leagues of the swarm behind.

They smoked together protectively, as if to secure themselves against any strolling party of robbers before the arrival of reinforcements. The Pawnee Republican well knew the passion for praise that is so very vehement in the Fair Sex, and he garnished Puss Titter in the usual tasty way as she posed for him eagerly, mindful that such admiration had become a surprise elegance in their ignorant age.

Still, such compliments were of no importance to the rest of the world, and wholly unallied to the hallucinations of mad people.

The Pawnee Republican drew close, infamous in his morals and actions, the appetite of his lean smile wafting toward her through the washed out smoke. The kiss came unexpectedly, like warfare from a government without courage forced to carry out the wishes of its mad sovereign. The keen cold air sharpened Puss Titter's appetite and she felt a delectable ecstasy as their motions swaddled together in Saturn's white light.

The air seemed a quiverful of clear melody as they enjoyed the memorable nocturne.

Suddenly a group came tumbling into the passageway, struggling as if blinded by demons they had ceased to worship. From the midst of the swirling recreants Ms. Like Awesome attempted to join Puss Titter and The Pawnee Republican, but the vacuum left behind sucked her back into the horde. The whole crew hurtled together, seemingly aimless in its consumptive self-entertainment, and Puss Titter dragged the gentlewoman from the midst of the rabble, causing a roar of violent outrage. But it hardly mattered, once free of the mob the MILF collapsed, the thud of her fall like thunder in an unpolished dystopia.

It was apparent that the tinsel bravery of the evening had collected its dues.

Puss Titter tried bombast, threats and flattery to persuade her friend to rise, but it was of little use. The MILF was out cold, the recreational injury of her alcoholic stupor as impossible to reverse as an obscene story told at a child's bedtime. When Puss Titter looked back for The Pawnee Republican she saw that he had vanished like a man released from the arc of a dishonorable and corroding debt, taking the clot of toroidal poseurs with him.

The peripheral attributes of the episode ascended with a dry resistance in the alley's uncomfortable equilibrium.

When Puss Titter finally managed to lead Ms. Like Awesome to the street, she felt as though they were the only strangers in a town of two natives. As the pair got in a cab, trusting the driver to lead them safely through the shadow of fate, the desolation of the scene was only increased by the selfish vacancies they left behind.

A REEKING APOSTATE

The Pawnee Republican sat on a bench in the little orchard adjoining Cherry Draws Beat's cottage and watched the trees put out their mossy arms to embrace the motionless shade. He suppressed his instinct to squash a rugged cockchafer going about its arboreal tedium, having learned some time ago to neither let a proud man come nigh God nor let God come nigh a proud man. Instead, he felt an inclination to avoid the vain and contentious suits arising from nature's laws and maintained his admiration of such slow motion violence from a distance.

The man stopped in his works when Cherry Draws Beat approached, the interrupter apparently reserving herself for future interruption as she gave The Pawnee Republican a sheet of notebook paper. This handwritten page, with letters like small filaments of silver that have somehow struggled out of a stream, was Cherry Draws Beat's reply to an email that she had been handed earlier in the day.

The Pawnee Republican smiled licorously and with a mountainous sound walked up the path toward the chamber in her dwelling where he kept his own portable computer. Once there he fulfilled his duty like a horseman's willing mount then sifted through Cherry Draws Beat's inbox, each chat following the squeeze of its provoking questionnaire. The Pawnee Republican held the belief that he had been given a divine mission and so, like a lesser god irritated by having to attend to the needs of some inept species, he began fascistically deleting worthless emails.

Then an unexpected cue rose like a crimson pennon provoking those with their hands already dueling. An email had arrived as he sat there, delivered without provocation or consent, its subject enhanced by a dexterous promise of shimmering wealth:

```
From: UK Lottery Organization
To: Whom it may concern
Subject: You have won the sweeptakes!
Reply-To: Thaumast@trudgepigsails.biz


Beloved owner of this stately email address,
be merry and joyful this day as the result of
the UK lottery online e-mail address free-
ticket winning draws held in Bangkok Thailand
has just been released and we are delighted
to pronounce that your email address won you
the sum of 4.6 Million!
Just in case you are thinking of how you won
without entering, then realize again that
this contest of the UK Lottery Organization
in which you have emerged as a prosperous
champion was an online draw, and your email
address entitles you to claim the bona fide
sum.
```

You are to contact me, Mr. Thaumast Trudgepig,
on the above email address for swift delivery
of your highcoped and breathtaking cheque of
4.6 Million and MAKE SURE you include the
below listed information:

The current geographic location of your hut/
residence and such homespun address where you
wish to receive either your valid certified
cashiers bank cheque of 4.6 Million or CASH.

Applauding you by one hand, Mr. Thaumast
Trudgepig

The Pawnee Republican instantly suspected that it was another indistinct promise from some Spam Bot unable to make a single movement naturally. Nothing would be easier than to delete it but he hesitated, perhaps this one was different. After all, not every hundred-dollar bill is phony and The Pawnee Republican certainly didn't want to be another pale and frightened man watching the sailing ship of opportunity pass by. There could be a human source, such unexpected things did happen, he had read about them.

As he wavered, the very vehemence of the plot that held possession of him grew in strength, and with it, his cunning. Cherry Draws Beat had no need for the 4.6 million; she had a salary and students that would do anything to graduate. The Pawnee Republican had only food, charcoal and cardiac complications; it was time to give his life a fresh extension. After all, to leave such prospects unanswered would only lead to dead bodies, and the Pawnee Republican certainly wanted to avoid their company.

The Pawnee Republican would take Cherry Draws Beat's fortune for his own, for all employees secretly want to live in their superior's house on the hill. So, with his heart pounding like the pulse of a techno beat in the chest of a teenager on Ecstasy, The Pawnee Republican responded:

```
From: The Pawnee Republican
To: Thaumast Trudgepig
Subject: A proper kind of answer!
Reply-To:Dr.LawyerIndianChief@pawnshopinjun.com

Dearest Mr. Thaumast Trudgepig, who has saved
my life from an unsure closure, allow me to
be direct, pointed and aphoristic, but never
merely suggestive. Tears of joy ran down
my cheeks upon receipt of your email and
consequently I will avoid any descantations
that would deny me this new found gold. I have
no suspicions, for after all, only an idiot
would trip over the digital trail of motives
behind such a welcoming questionnaire.
Please assure your men that I am in proper
condition to perform.
I was born in a wildly disheveled bed under
a great arc of stone but now reside along
with all the other fellows in a neighborhood
where an indistinct rumor of them lives to
this day. My mail is delivered to The Satyr's
Sojourn in the Holy Farces district of Hill
Town Eye.
```

Please contact me again when you have the
time and instruments to spare.

Compiling   the   depositions,   The   Pawnee
Republican

Outside the room, nature continued to coat the
instrumental world with its choral sheen as the daylight
extracted the garden from its shadows. But The Pawnee
Republican drew the curtains closely together as if he had
been imprisoned, ignoring the cultivated state of the land.
Once again his progress toward integrity had stalled at the
pitfall of greed, and he sat in the cymbal glimpse of the
room's twilight considering his own bad company. Even
though The Pawnee Republican had learned to cope with
the remorse he felt for his self-indulgences, he still felt like
a reeking apostate, and nothing would exonerate him from
the guilt of his disregard for the agreement he had with
Cherry Draws Beat.

The Pawnee Republican had experienced the
government's idea of repentance before and he had no
plans to return to the constrictive dive of detention.
Nevertheless, Mr. Thaumast Trudgepig provided eloquent
grounds for yet another shady undertaking. Assuming that
the identity theft was successful, The Pawnee Republican
would spend vulgar decades in unreserved rapture, never
again forced to consider another distortion of his duty to

other people. However, if he failed, tragedy would submit the most grievous and dreadful sufferings.

He contemplated all the risks and miseries and swore that he would make up for this treasonous incident by giving to charity like Ju Lai, who fed the hungry birds with his own flesh.

But until then there was correspondence to attend to, as if all the world's intellectuals depended on such articulate declarations to secure themselves a large circle of friends. The Pawnee Republican returned to work and quickened his pace, like a horse that has caught its first scent of home, knowing that where there is smoke there is not necessarily fire: there can also be a country mansion as calm and snug as ever.

THE PROPHYLACTIC DIGRESSION

The morning's expected style was just beginning as Puss Titter crossed the street and headed to the nourishing chaos of The Metal Crossroads Café. She pictured the robots in the buildings around her rising from their untroubled sleep with the first comprehensions of the day, as if they were postulants eagerly applying for consciousness. Soon the streets of Hill Town Eye would be like rivers full of salmon reeling upstream toward the capitalist machines that had given them birth.

They were not humanists interested in the substance of the news or current outbursts of indignation; an eventless and ordered life suited them best.

As Puss Titter nursed her hangover in the café, she concentrated on checking her email to avoid eye contact with the surrounding flock of ostentatious domestics at their breakfasts, each of whom appeared quite prepared to die without leaving even a diminutive inheritance to their fellow robots. Bolt worshippers, nature jerks and paltry boys sat at mirrored tables, released from the corroding debt of their customary servitude by the tender progress of their degradation. These were amateurs of art and the picturesque, gnawing at each other like red mice that destroy seeds before they can grow.

As Puss Titter logged on to the email account of her construct Oriflamme Plowjobber, the immensity of her dishonesty horrified her and she almost wished she had sent Dude Noway a message of warning instead. She knew that what he could accomplish socially with one idea was remarkable, so it was with urgent curiosity that she read his pornographic concordat:

```
From: Dude Noway
To: Oriflamme Plowjobber
Subject: A Sudden Acquaintance!
Reply-To: DudeNoWay@RattledSwilldown.net
```

```
WTF Oriflamme, arent this just stupid? My
wife enhanced her boobs to D size but forgot
how to make an eatable dinner and now I have
to look at her pervert body... and eat trash-
burgers? Hell, I fukced her after I spit all
that out! I told her mother that her daughter
was made for fukcing, not cooking! And guess
what I saw next — a fat guy taking a skinny,
blond slut from behind then putting his arm
up her butt hole till his elbow… and all
this crazy shit happening next to an opened
window.
Look, I know you need my help, you want to
do that too but you can't — so I can fcuk
her instead of you, yes, watch the process,
no problem! Sex on your behalf- thats not
cheating, agree?
Come on, I want to look at your awesome
body... have you done anything like that,
```

```
sexy beast? Tell me if you really want to
follow me next time I go there!

Pumped early, Dude Noway

P.S. I have no plans for the week, FYI
```

The shock of this treacherous campaign brought Puss Titter to her feet and she shook her fists, which appeared like two opposing jets in midair battle. As anger vibrated through her soul, Puss Titter vowed that her revenge would be more immediate than any act of God, and she swore to reveal Dude Noway as just another self-indulgent shit, feeding on the bodies of his companions and vibrating off the fat of the land.

The uncomfortable patrons near Puss Titter sat waiting for her to keel over, fearing that they had perhaps ordered "Drunk Lady" as their main course.

Finally Puss Titter sat down, reminded that childhood is seldom bright and womanhood mostly sad and fretful, proving merely the pointlessness of reimagining the margin between them. But something in her had undergone a much greater change than she realized, even though the numbness was now gone and the keen air had sharpened her appetite for vengeance. It wasn't Dude Noway's ownerless infidelity that bothered Puss Titter, her lament was that Dude Noway thought he had some underhanded ability that would enable him to cheat on her and she would never suspect his prophylactic digression. As is usually the case with betrayal, he had underestimated her, and that audacity filled her with anger.

It made no difference to Puss Titter that the chicanery was all her doing, and perhaps this ruse of hers was just a way to discover the purpose of her life, or if it was bereft of any meaning at all. Unfortunately for her, the answer might be prompt and plain and ever within hearing, but she would never see the dawning of its light.

Puss Titter drew her pelt of kittenish horsecloth closer around her shoulders and began a reply to Dude Noway's anarchic contract, typing like a spurned leader canvassing for a mandate:

```
From: Oriflamme Plowjobber
To: Dude Noway
Subject: The Great Cocks Crusade!
Reply-To: Oriflamme@straponfiesta.com


Hey Dude, good news! Its not just me anymore,
all my durable girlfriends are now hooked up
and these dominant females are out for their
own pleasure. Nothing makes them happier than
hearing a bloke scream dog-ear for mercy.
And that's not all, my girlfriends videos
feature chicks with rubber cocks protruding
on  or  else  after  their  pelvis.  Imagine
watching  that  on  bigscreen!  You'll  wish
you were the one  finished at that moment,
violated in each way you can think.
That's what our Strapon Fiesta will be, not
just some customary porn occurrence!
Meet  me  Saturday  night  at  The  Opprobrium
```

```
Lounge, you will know me by the strength of
my character. XOXOXO

Aim for the mouth, Oriflamme
```

The falsetto greatness of the bogus email filled Puss Titter with luxurious pride and she was sure that her future letters would further tempt Dude Noway. But that wasn't the point; after all, he was supposed to reject the advances of Oriflamme Plowjobber, not succumb to them. Puss Titter felt her inspiring glow fade like the capital assets of a country bargain. Once she had thought that love could never die, but now she was sure that in this world nothing endures, eventually everything is conquered and subdued. As Puss Titter looked about the café and studied its crew, she realized that she too was no longer the voice of life, merely its faint echo.

HELL BANKNOTES

Hill Town Eye was considered by many to be an outpost of a civilization in a hurry to be gone, making life for its inhabitants a slow starvation. The city's uncompromising refusal to accept its future of sunless days made it attractive to outsiders, and alien rockets clogged the streets like a mighty avalanche that has filled a hidden gorge.

Within the city limits, flesh might never realize corporeal form and remain turning in the mind, as if on a honeymoon trip where nothing is ever unpacked.

In Saturday's twilight the sachem Falling Bong Water stood out front of the bus station with his excellent teeth secured, describing the vital processes of growth, metabolism, and contractility to a temporary congregation of onlookers. He believed that most people would die alone and unsaved in their hospital beds, their eternal rest made a mockery of as a winter rain beat pitilessly on their graves. The thought fired his fervor but he still seemed unable to alert the consciences of men or the psychic butter of women.

Nothing that he could say to his crowd would help them, yet hope would fain take his heart to swear that he could.

The figure of a man in light armor stood partly hidden among the audience, as if confined by his inability to escape. It was The Pawnee Republican, whose strange and urgent guise seemed altogether natural for his recent course of deceit. Previous exploits had taught him that even unrealized sums of money have a restless time of it and a holstered revolver slapped against his thigh. Indeed, if there entered any one who was a stranger to the merits of such, it could only be one who had never been trained by trial.

Meanwhile, two old ladies circled the gathering while handing out Hell Banknotes, a fictional currency to be used as legal tender should one arrive in Hell after death. The eldest presented The Pawnee Republican with several, guessing correctly that he was the sort that might need them, but he kept his hands at his sides and looked away. She shoved several in his shirt pocket before moving past like a vessel falling rapidly astern, as if she understood his indifference.

The Pawnee Republican had learned long ago that God declined to protect him, and not even commands issued word for word could affect his purpose in the opposite direction.

Eventually the eyes and thoughts of the listening crowd wandered beyond the blue Highlands and the two natives were left alone together in the street with nothing other than what has been described. As to the governance of their tongues in respect to the matter of Cherry Draws Beat, The Pawnee Republican had only arrived to thank Falling Bong Water for his employment, intending to leave the matter of Thaumast Trudgepig and the lottery winnings unspoken. But, as is often the case with good fortune, he found it impossible to keep the matter undisclosed. So, after solemnly plighting his troth to secrecy, Falling Bong Water read a copy of the most recent email:

From: Thaumast Trudgepig
To: The Pawnee Republican
Subject: Highcoped spodizators!
Reply-To: Thaumast@trudgepigsails.biz

Cherished Mr. Pawnee Republican, thank you
for the completed bio-data form, including
the habitat where your 4.6 Million is to be
delivered.
Please pardon me for not having the pleasure
of knowing your mindset before my response to
your last reply regarding your 4.6 Million.
I know within me that nothing ventured is
nothing gained and that success and riches
never come easy on a platter of gold. But
investigations, which were afterwards made,
will bring to light that you won 4.6 Million
without effort!
All that is required from you to ensure the
delivery of your winnings is a one time
payment of $3500USD for the paper works,
take note of that.
Consequently, I sent you this mail without
a measure of fear, but if you release the

```
necessary $3500USD disbursement, I will
initiate this process towards a conclusion
and you can spent your 4.6 Million.

Bobbing reasonably, Thaumast Trudgepig
```

The two natives decided to celebrate by downing firewater at The Satyr's Sojourn as if it were a military command. As the pair walked past the eloquent trees promoting their haven of rest in Domesday Park, The Pawnee Republican realized he would be expected to buy the drinks. Such involuntary largesse was something that he hadn't foreseen and he felt his joy fading like a whispered catastrophe. He had anticipated rolling in the fat of his prosperity as he jammed millions into tech-based bank lobbies, but that might not be so. After all, it was his greed that had led him to deceive Cherry Draws Beat and it could be the gluttony of others that brought about his downfall.

They passed an elderly beggar whose meager habit resembled a conical tent with the end of a shoot for its top. His head was large and square, like a block of wood, reminiscent of collections of vegetable matter that have been washed down from the eminences above. Even the deformed ground upon which the madman stood made him appear impaled on misfortune, and he seemed confused and fleeting as his filthy fingers clutched the coins in his palm like clustering branches.

The Pawnee Republican decided no tiresome prudence could ever again convince him that wealth was an affliction.

Inside The Satyr's Sojourn, dark forms toiled away in an onslaught of depravity, as though a pill had purged off all their scruples. Since The Pawnee Republican's last visit, the saloon's unity of purpose had declined deeper into anarchy and unnamability, each perversion seeming like a philippic against a despised god. Onstage, Dixi Nutshell was down to her g-string, wildly swinging her renowned breasts as several officers shouted orders, their voices keyed to the DJ. Fortunately, Falling Bong Water had the tavern's network of wormeaten debauchery charted to an inch, and years of liberal activity throughout the boroughs had given him the shoulders and the heart of a tiger. As the pair passed through the brocaded discharge to reach the bar, he drubbed the losers out of their way with the fierce desperation of a poisoned king.

Saturday night blew by in a pattern of impolitic conversation, The Pawnee Republican's inventive paternosters a poached counterpoint to Falling Bong Water's bacchanalian rap. Other drunks made themselves of the party, each lost soul a hell unto itself, and at one point a misunderstood comment had The Pawnee Republican's instant death a short six inches off. Even so, the tempest seemed to give more pleasure than pain to the two natives as they rode out the constant waves of marauders that wished to sustain and cheer them on.

As closing time neared, The Pawnee Republican realized that Falling Bong Water had mysteriously disappeared and left him to cope with the towering debt.

He felt that even in proportion to his new means, he had contributed more than his share to the chaos, so he threw one of the Hell Banknotes on the bar and pushed his way through the mob to escape out the back door. As The Pawnee Republican lurched down the alley, it was obvious to any observer that he had no qualifications that could single him out for a more hopeful future. But even so, one would make a great mistake to suppose that he could sink no lower than he already had.

A LONG SPELL BETWEEN FUCKS

That same Saturday night also marked the beginning of the week long Festival of Territorial Usurpation, and some of the revelers in the crowds waved their arms in defiance of the rules while others were content to loiter idly, lacking the spirit of even the smallest animal that crawls. Most of the clubbing wives had been driven into vice by their husbands, scarce showing themselves throughout the day as they waited for night to awaken the perversions that their mothers had denied themselves in different times.

Stately, solemn, sad, withdrawn, baffled, mad, turbulent, feeble, the faces on the laughing heads were emphasized like hundreds of caricatures in some horrid exhibition.

Puss Titter pushed through the clots of human pleurisy like an aeronaut who has planned to cross the sea by night, the crowds reminding her of Guinea chickens clamoring their satisfaction at nothing. She was on her way to The Opprobrium Lounge, where Ms. Like Awesome already sat in full character as the dildo dominatrix Oriflamme Plowjobber, waiting in her tilt and tournament for Dude Noway to arrive. Puss Titter planned to watch their liaison from a distance, just as the sun pours into the crystal of a grape, anticipating the moment that she would reveal herself, complete and ideal, to shame Dude Noway.

When Puss Titter finally made it through the narrow entrance of The Opprobrium Lounge and settled in at her vantage point, she reread a print out she had made earlier of Dude Noway's scandalous reply to Oriflamme Plowjobber's last email:

```
From: Dude Noway
To: Oriflamme Plowjobber
Subject: An unlucky planker!
Reply-To: DudeNoWay@RattledSwilldown.net


Heeey Oriflamme… Did you hear that I got nude
during some bitches bikini photo shoot? It
was fantastic! I used my one eyed monster
on that always drunk bitch even though she's
my best buddy! She (thanks to her, right???)
captured on her Samsung how I did it and
you should have seen my genitalias after
that amazing sexual experience! On that same
weekend I also participated in the first
anniversary cheerleader's nude run, what a
blast!
Hey, I know you want to make your stunningly
sexy strokes in the asylum of my butt since I
know nothing makes you happier than hearing
a slave's lament at the Strapon Fiesta!
Anyway, get ready for a high resolution;
mind blowing festivity cause I'll be there
at The Opprobrium Lounge, oh crazy ducktale!
```

See you then, you sexy cheeks, Dude Noway

P.S. Did you know that I use to be some kind
of exotic movie actor? You, my next star,
should know me and my job! I want to show
you how I lick my own…! Maybe you should
try your talent in that hot business since
the central subject is fukcing, thats sexy,
right?

When Puss Titter had first received the email, she felt as if manure had been flung in her face at the very gates of Eden. All the vexations and sorrows that usually harass the mind were rolled and folded and put away to make room for these new troubling thoughts, and she laughed at the darkness while clenching her despairing hands out of sight.

Puss Titter understood that Dude Noway had wanted to craft a grand description of himself, such as might endure to the end of time, and for this reason he had taken on a depraved form. None of his claims of perversion were true, that she knew, but most men who are masters of their own career resort to such deceit. Complacent people are the same drag on a society as a brake on a wheel and Dude Noway's psychic agitation was an attack on a world that he could neither tolerate nor endure. But perhaps the wages of sin were high enough to give him a margin for amusement; after all, Man, the suffering inflictor, sails on sufferance directed by a steady hand.

The time passed like a long spell between fucks.

Suddenly the geographical distribution of the room was punctuated by a violent agitation as Dude Noway whirled in from his battle against the thievish fray outside, his noisome marrow and black eyes conspiring like twin plagues. He wore a stone fleece over his lash charged robe, as if the tempestuous struggle between Popery and Protestantism had been resumed in the streets. But even with this heroism there was little good to be expected of him: like some torpid jester, a disorderly harness hung around his neck, indicating that he was ready to comply with all of Oriflamme Plowjobber's chastening demands.

Puss Titter wanted to cry aloud but was unable to articulate a sound as thoughts unutterable roared with a portentous thunder through her mind. Although she had engineered this deception, she still felt that Dude Noway had wronged her intolerably, and even in the weakness of her desolation she was ready to beat the breath and life out of him.

It was an inflexible fatality by virtue of that which has to be.

Dude Noway peered about in search of Oriflamme Plowjobber, expecting that the novelty of the situation would make her obvious to him, but it was her voice that finally brought them together. With a selfish declaration she called to him, confirming her superior position by demanding his rapid arrival to her address and, just as faults, mistakes, and embarrassment in the conduct of any open warfare put one combatant above the other, he acquiesced with no delay.

Ms. Like Awesome stood tanned, lined, and fitted with buckles, as unattainable as any beautiful woman in a remote country. She was well suited for her role as Oriflamme Plowjobber, and her tempting thicket of black hair shone with a red glare like the blood of a dragon slain coming from the clouds. She was built to destroy the old representations of God, conveying divinity with the magnificence of her cleavage, perfect in the opinion of all anatomists. The thrust of her assumed imperiousness had been reserved strictly for Dude Noway, but Ms. Like Awesome enjoyed ruling her own empire as she stood resolute in honor of her own legend. She relished her new identity, and for the time being the only name to which she would answer was Oriflamme.

Conveying her superiority by maintaining a face of profound disinterest, she appeared cold and distant from the ideas of touch favored by most fully developed men.

Dude Noway stood still for a moment gazing blankly now, as if at his diary sealed up in a barrel. He knew that, like a prize poem, which is memorized but only occasionally recited, he would seldom be able to reveal this night's fearsome gush of adventure for other's enjoyment. Worse, confined within that arrowy net like birds within a cage, his secret might fade until it was as if nothing had ever happened. After all, time destroys everything that it does not sanctify.

He moved blindly through the vacant space toward

her as if he were a fish on a line and nothing could avert his barbarous doom.

When they finally stood face to face, Oriflamme Plowjobber put a finger to Dude Noway's lips, forcing him to silence. Neither spoke, as if the memory of some unfortunate phrase had obliterated their capacity to perform such a task. As Dude Noway stared up at Oriflamme Plowjobber in amazement, he appeared to her like a beast that might yet carry out the wishes of a sovereign who could only be entertained by its slaughter. Yet a glow of expectation seemed to enclose them as they concentrated upon the moment at hand, inspiring a fresh extension in the range of their consciousness; indeed, Oriflamme Plowjobber had decided to put a scheme into action that would eliminate Puss Titter's planned intervention altogether. The pair would make their escape to some forlorn hotel by the seaside, surrounded only by red heather and salt winds. There they could abandon themselves to the versatility and variety of their depravity, enjoying a memorable nocturne in the realm of beds, bending themselves into curious knots like porn cooks in a PVC tiled kitchen.

The Opprobrium Lounge was now packed with drunken men who had left the Black Republic of Texas carrying picks and shovels and were engaged in the sort of conduct that maddens to crime. From this melee Oriflamme Plowjobber and Dude Noway escaped unnoticed by Puss Titter, well content to go whither the path might lead them, whether their steps were on that long road to Calvary or through the door of a dungeon.

When at last Puss Titter realized the lovers' getaway, she felt like a great fire extinguished by a hundred winds and draughts down the chimney. But although a tear or two could without much coaxing be induced to hop from her eyes, she bore Dude Noway's infidelity with a distressed resignation; it was Ms. Like Awesome's treachery that beat the breath and life out of her. Puss Titter knew of a no more striking picture of desolation than that presented by a treacherous friend and she felt led astray by behests and encompassed with lies. In her mind there were loud clamourings for the arrest of the traitor, but once her skepticism had made itself uncomfortably clear, she knew that she would have to play not only the deputy but also the executioner.

THE HOTEL DEMIREP

The **Pawnee Republican** made it from The Satyr's Sojourn to Domesday Park before collapsing on the grass as if he was a scuttled soul dumped in an unmarked grave. In the night sky above him the satellites blazed forth under the stars like supposititious letters of gratitude crumpled up and added to a blaze, tolling away his life as they had tolled away epochs. The different manifestations of the Festival of Territorial Usurpation spun around him and the sounds of merriment grew quite too bad to bear; never did the earth seem so unquiet. But The Pawnee Republican finally slept, a fur cloak muffled around him as he rocked in his linden cradle, much in the same way that an honest man backs out of a loophole.

As the swift night grew deep The Pawnee Republican commenced to dream, and in that world he performed his egocentic part:

He was running through semitropical plants in the glow of a desert sunset, dragging a skull furiously behind him as smoke billowed from the spot where He had begun his flight. Two men detached themselves from a log cabin chinked with mud and blew down the dirty street after Him, peppering everything with dust as they shouted English poetry. On came the figures, their long arms tapering to hands with miniature gun barrels for fingers, the frightful organs blazing. Ahead of Him a signal light gleamed and He made a bound, half leaping and half falling in the strange radiance which had filled the boulevard. But the long straight reach seemed to pivot on its centre and suddenly He was sliding through halls and over flights of steps into a large hall filled with a great crowd of people. They wore graceful black and white costumes, suspiciously adorned from head to foot with mirrors, celluloid bureau sets, flower seeds, and rubber toys. Rain fell thickly as females and children flew in the heavens, which had turned green in the growing darkness. In a small garden with a fountain in the middle, He came upon a group of cupids, all dressed in cambric and holding cocked pistols as they surrounded a brass kettle decked with flowers. Inside He could see a golden object covered with silky roots of white hair boiling in sacrificial wine and making the sound of an applauding crowd. Cherry Draws Beat, crowned with orchids and clutching a mechanical creature to her breast passed Him as the cat Akron pedaled behind her on a white and purple bicycle from which were sold newspapers, twine and penny bottles of ink. The courtyard disappeared and became a row of tired old houses extending to infinity as an execution platoon reloading its arms made its way toward Him through a steady cloud of smoke and flame. He fled with a showy trot past the fruit and foliage of the surrounding villages, the pavement snatching at His shoes as he ran. Suddenly His name appeared, painted perpendicularly on a glass light in the lobby of The Impervious Hotel where miniature villages and ships, burnt, plundered, and destroyed by some unseen force were piled under a rude shelter. Puss Titter, dressed as an oracle and wearing pendants of beautiful jewels around her throat, approached Him by the downstairs lagoon of the hotel and kissed His face up and down, too insistent to be ignored. He held her hand as they passed down a corridor and opened the first door without hesitation. Something very beautiful and valuable floated halfway between the floor and roof, its superior radiance of wisdom and virtue illuminating a small exhibit in the temple of Apollo on the Palatine, the atrium filled with blacks, mulattoes and famous Indian fighters that saluted them with three volleys of small arms. He leapt out of a window into the strange pageant of clouds burning light and commenced flying above Hill Town Eye, his hands covered by red worsted mittens edged with white.

Sunday morning came. The breakfasts were eaten, the camps broken and The Pawnee Republican woke to the spray of the lawn sprinklers in Domesday Park's playing fields. Exhaling the delightful odor of vegetation, he staggered from the square, stumbling on like the bitter getting fit and putting forth to sea. His progress through the pageant's roaming flesh was remarkable only for the shrinking courtesy of his rude passage, and he ignored the string of curses that followed him. As The Pawnee Republican listened to the Festival of Territorial Usurpation's sounds of merriment, his temporary companions gathered about him with faces that implied his staying away would have been remarked upon. Runners straggled by from previous races, asking him why he was so late, never once noticing anything suggestive of his mental corruption.

Yet even in his sodden and sorry state, the meaning of his dream was clear to The Pawnee Republican: he must send Thaumast Trudgepig the required $3500 immediately. If he did not, the framework of his good fortune would crumble with a theatric sense of painted distress. His financial infirmity was a ponderous stone of bundled debt, and the thought of more years in the prison of pauperism pounded like a work boot on his brain. So, as he was aware already that nothing left is a very indifferent companion, to such an extent that he was tempted to connive and swindle, he vowed to find the money.

And find the money he did, although it was just one of the Hell Banknotes shoved in his shirt pocket by the old woman at Falling Bong Water's sermon the day before.

The Pawnee Republican threw it down and continued his lazy tour, the crowd growing denser, like natives turned out to see an elephant killed. He stepped aside to avoid three Swedeland queers, each stamped with the same signet of perfection, and collided with Puss Titter, whom he had not seen since their drinkspiller at The Faecal Breech days before. The two stood there in shock, as if waiting for summoned witnesses to arrive.

She could still feel against her skin the rough warm stuff of his coat.

He appeared confused and fleeting.

Puss Titter's handful of wayward charm and red lips concealed the wrecking business she was about.

His jacket's graceful plaid of varied hue obscured the mud and leaves from his night in Domesday Park.

They spoke loudly but their conversation was obliterated by the crowd's engines and clapping hands. Events were going on at that end of the square so they moved together with great determination toward The Metal Crossroads Café and were soon in their own little sanctum enjoying the tournament of their mutual interrogations. It was at this moment, whatever any Irish party may say, that the light of mutual attraction again sprang up between them like a product that has risen to an excessive price.

But before proceeding any further, there was one thing that had to be gotten out of the way lest their imaginations become tamed.

The Pawnee Republican booked a room for them on the Grand Rue at the Hotel Demirep, a skin warehouse wrapped in its own expensive mystery. Their bathroom's in-mirror television showed the musical fountain by the pool below so he drew the curtains and turned for a backward glance at Puss Titter standing there in her delightful nakedness. Her bangs fell upon her brow as she floated with a transcendent simplicity across the room into his manly seduction, fawning low in appreciation of his attention. They had not the civil restraint of marriage so he invaded her like a convoy reaching some disputed colony, reveling in their catholicity and sureness of style. All this time not a word was spoken; indeed, no Latin versification would make any considerable difference in their pleasure which was as rich as Greek to be also as musical. They were twin planets teeming with life, where honeysuckles, ripened by the sun, perfume each great sphere with sensual overindulgence.

To an observer this positive ordeal would have appeared to be a contest without provocation, each combatant attempting to discover what the other's tongue was like at its furthest end.

Their passion was sharp and their fancy luxuriant, but soon their folly timed out and they both fell back repaired and restored in their rapturous contentment. It was as if the two of them had descended from the mirror over the bed and now broadcast the splendor of a heavenly light, one that showed far more clearly than before how no other friendship had ever been interrupted by more ardent feelings.

Still, as the lovers lay with their eyes closed to rest undisturbed within their ramparts of bed sheets, they would both would have done well to paste a memorandum of this moment inside their diadems, for it is only a saint's privilege to remember the past clearly enough to repeat it.

A DIMENSIONAL TREASURE

Dude Noway and Oriflamme Plowjobber drove through the Saturday night darkness like youthful minstrels on the moonlight flung, listening to classic rock and looking in the direction whence they supposed they proceeded. They drank beer and muscatel, consumed sweets, and paid florid attention to one another, relishing and appreciating their high order of roundheaded lechery.

Finally the first part of their descent lay behind them and the pair stood in their hotel room demesne, toasting one another with champagne as they each took a hit of ecstacy. Dude Noway was so confounded with anticipation that his words got mixed until he became speechless and he could only utter a heartfelt cry of relief when Oriflamme Plowjobber gave him a blue lozenge shaped pill, blew him a kiss from the bedroom and slammed the door shut in his face.

It was apparent that affection in the guise of hostilities would soon commence.

Still, the fury of passion which had led Ms. Like Awesome to betray Puss Titter was wearing off, and the blood which had surged to her brain now stood away from her own impulsive nature. As she slipped into her high heels, she realized that the purpose of her role as Oriflamme Plowjobber was to penalize Dude Noway for his sins even as he committed them. The crime itself would be his punishment, and Oriflamme Plowjobber was doing Puss Titter a favor by breaking Dude Noway in advance of his comeuppance. Besides, Oriflamme Plowjobber relished the idea of violating Dude Noway for the sins of all the men who had ever given her complaint. Her studied, sly, ensnaring arts would close the performance and eliminate him from any further consideration.

Meanwhile, Dude Noway sat nude and wet on a couch in the living room, listening to Wrath Radio on the television and rereading an email from that morning on his handheld:

> From: Oriflamme Plowjobber
> To: Dude Noway
> Subject: Your penis deserves a better life!
> Reply-To: Oriflamme@straponfiesta.com
>
> OMG Dude! This is BIG DISCOVERY for me! Really! Yeah, some sexy woman from New York, dressed like a Snowman, tried to bring ecstasy inside my apartment! WELL, thanks to Holy Christ, that S.W.A.T. arrested that crazy bitch and took her to jail (without underwear!!!) and left the E, but only enough for us! So now you and me gained some extra load and are gonna get to know how to become skilled Rabitators! And guess what

else? You'll be a horny giant Viagron coz my
precious adviser left a boner pill by Pfizer
too!

Embrace the means, Oriflamme Plowjobber

BTW, have you ever seen yourself in a ladies
bra? No? Well, it doesn't mean that you
are gay since you are punk a hipster or
something like that.. bla, bla, bla.. So
lets associate this shit up and put you in
girls underwear too!

This email had plunged Dude Noway into a daylong
frenzy of pornographic anticipation, but now that their
covenant was about to be realized he felt a smutty unease.
After all, this wasn't his fetish; Oriflamme Plowjobber
had approached him with the scenario as though she was
making cattle do what they particularly did not want to.
But as the drugs came on and he began to get that certain
feeling of all those dolphins, like, swimming through his
blood stream, his hopes returned. Dude Noway sank back
into the cushions to watch the light throb, reviewing his
depraved fantasies as the atmosphere of the room around
him began to accelerate to match the techno music. The
furniture began to migrate into the distance, silently,
deliberately, as if with a mammalian consciousness.

He sat in the catching bacterium, motionless and
dumbfounded by the flashes of light, disguising his inward
qualms with an outward calm.

The door opened and Oriflamme Plowjobber strutted into the room, her strapon swaying like some perverted divining rod. The harassed look in her eyes had given way to an expression of icy-cold arrogance and she posed like a dimensional treasure, enjoying a wild pride in her own beauty. She commanded Dude Noway to his knees with a spoken shot and he helplessly obeyed, creeping hesitantly toward her across the carpet.

He lay humbly before Oriflamme Plowjobber, pecking at her high heels like a deprived chicken boiling and heaving at her feet.

Oriflamme Plowjobber slid into the evil hyperspace of their reckless sex knowing full well that might without mercy is tyranny. Dude Noway was just some unfinished creature servicing a queen, and there would be no pay for his slave labor other than her approval. Her miraculous disdain for him gave her body an unconquerable power and she forced his head onto her strapon, tugging at Dude Noway and jerking it in his mouth.

The Indian's senses were already overwhelmed when Oriflamme Plowjobber seized him by his hair and with a stern and determined grip forced him around. It was clear that his stapon banquet had been merely the prelude to a much more barbarous ingestion and Dude Noway's cries vibrated through the being of his tormentor as if he was her prey being torn to pieces. Raging in his toils, Dude Noway felt much like an innocent left at haphazard in a lawless land; there was no one with influences serene that could save him. He struggled against her wellfavoured skin but it wasn't long until his reserves came tumbling out as she demanded.

Soundless above them the banners of motes just stirred to the music.

In the stream of his thoughts Dude Noway felt the prostitution of his spirit, yet throughout the abasement it seemed to him that the whole event was a necessary phase and mood of his existence. Even so, such dreams must pass away, and as Oriflamme Plowjobber pulled back he knew that he surely could have found no lower depths elsewhere.

******

Dude Noway awoke Sunday afternoon in the tapestried suite where other missing men had also spent so many nights. It seemed that the day's light was not from an actual sun but rather some kind of as yet unknown source, and beside him Ms. Like Awesome advertised her smug upgrade with what are generally considered elements of happiness. Grave moments of sedated thoughts passed, and he set his perceptions upon the crabbed repentances that are required to negotiate the domain of consciousness, but cruel imprints of the night before flashed before him, unworthy of his genius.

Still, even with all these latest additions to the stream of his thoughts, the seedy raiment of a scheme began to wrap itself around his brain.

Dude Noway was sure that Puss Titter knew none of his secrets, and in any case he would oppose every insinuation that he had been off philandering. Monday he would rush to Puss Titter and press flowers against her heart, blaming his absence on Daedalus Megistus, the Chief of the Mutant Corps, and claim that a scandalous carouse of drugs and heavy drinking had ended in a blackout.

His appealing helplessness would surely reverse her skepticism.

When it was time to go, Dude Noway felt as though he was leaving only his shadow behind him in apparent isolation. Soon the pair were on their way back to Hill Town Eye with nothing to breathe but streets, streets, streets. As Ms. Like Awesome and Dude Noway left behind the green swards that had been invisible the night before, few words passed between them, their silences deepened alike by the earnestness of their individual contrition. Indeed, neither one of them suspected that the other was praying for a similar forgiveness.

THE CEREBRAL ORATOR

On **Monday morning**, The Pawnee Republican arrived at the office of Cherry Draws Beat, ready for another beginning of his daily life in the human family.

The evening before he had taken advantage of his post-coital clarity of thought to consider his plans, but as The Pawnee Republican had gazed at the distant hills lording over the granges in the night, he had seen more than the glittering outline of the Bank of Hill Town Eye. Like a dramatist who employs archaeology on the stage, he had considered his morals and actions in the flood of light that accompanies inspiration and had decided to get Puss Titter to loan him the $3500 for Thaumast Trudgepig.

As he now sat at his desk, he knew that immediate action was called for, and any theories which remained inactive in this potential change of fortune were irrelevant. The Pawnee Republican was an exceptionally gifted cerebral orator of the speeches in his head, so he fixed himself on the purpose of his appeal and began:

From: The Pawnee Republican
To: Puss Titter
Subject: A loving exhortation!
Reply-To:Dr.LawyerIndianChief@pawnshopinjun.com

Darling Puss Titter, please excuse me for not having the gratification of being able to anticipate your frame of mind at the moment you read this.

Let us discuss the economical habits of a hardy and struggling race. This is the one truth I have learned: Tomorrow can live without the body, but the body can not live without tomorrow… And more importantly, the body cannot live without money.

So, as a man fitted for the performance of such a task, I present to you my request for a loan of $3500USD, which will be invested in an opportunity that will finally put me within reach of the rich.

In fact, as my gratitude for what is bestowed I guarantee to repay you twice what you have lent.

By refusing, it would be easy for you to crush the pride of my belief in you, but I think you may yield to my plea in a way that is not contrary to your nature. As I let this offer of mine commend itself pleasantly to you, please keep in mind that all such matters ought constantly to flow as easily as the rewards that will stem from your efforts.

Together with our contents, The Pawnee Republican

His rhetoric was couched with the respect due to a woman of her fashion; however The Pawnee Republican knew that he had not only little chance of a hearing, but every likelihood of being drubbed mercilessly for even thinking that he did. Normally such a reaction would prove merely how futile are the efforts of honesty and reason to improve one's station in life, but The Pawnee Republican could act the imploring persuader so ingeniously that he was sure he could convince Puss Titter to furnish the necessary instrument.

Outside the room, the daylight trekked past on its way from the sun's shrine of gold, illuminating the scenery with a glowing enthusiasm.

His wait for Puss Titter's reply was so excruciating that The Pawnee Republican sank back into his place with weak mutterings, yearning for the power and strength of silence which is invariably followed by a greater proportional outburst of elation. He possessed the reckless and evil courage of a soldier yet he felt unsettled and considered prayer, even though he had always attributed the creation of the world to different glaring absurdities and not some magnum dei. As far as The Pawnee Republican was concerned, there is no rational advantage to a belief in God; intelligence is the light of the world and the chief glory of man, not religion. He remained agnostic, regardless of his competence to arraign and convict on grounds other than the cavils of biblical criticism.

The Pawnee Republican was confident that he would not be passing through either of the entrances to Heaven or Hell.

In the corridor outside, he could hear some obscure individual blithely humming like a young and hitherto unknown actor in a modern panorama of the Babes in the Wood. As the time passed, the sun lay agreeably on the walls and scattered books of his room as if amidst the dull magnificence of Versailles, but The Pawnee Republican found the mixture of such domestic pleasantry and online uncertainty to be thoroughly unnerving. Finally his callused patience was rewarded, and with cheesecake excitement The Pawnee Republican opened Puss Titter's riposte:

From: Puss Titter
To: The Pawnee Republican
Subject: Lycoperdon pawnbrokers!
Reply-To: Puss@pusstitter.com

Seriously, Mister Republican… As you can see, you received this e-mail and opened it… and when you reply, I will be doing the same for you. This conduct is known as reciprocity, a tradition that arose with regard to Roman praises. Concerning so essential a point, there can be no objection to trusting that the mind of you, the reader of this email, will understand that where there is a reaching down, there is also a reaching up.
Even so, I dare not venture beyond this cryptic affair until my feeling's mysteries stand developed and yours are abruptly revealed.
My initial opinion was in favor of condemning your request but that would hardly be fair on a man who had made me feel better than any therapeutic metaphor. Still, a

confusing element in the whole question is:
What do you fear worse than poverty? You
need not undo your collar before answering,
just think clearly and remember that you
are addressing my generosity and humanity.

Evaded by that which I command, Puss Titter

P.S. My actions require that love and duty
become one... not a difficult task, but it is
what must be done.

The Pawnee Republican had suspected all along that the quickest way to her purse was through Puss Titter's heart, and her postscript confirmed his plot as a fact already accomplished. He was well prepared to affect the stance of a tender lover if it would deliver the final vote that would tip the scheme in his favor. But The Pawnee Republican knew how difficult it is for one to appreciate another's good luck and the fitness of things dictates that jealousy be mounted at the forward response and connivance at the aft. Consequently he would be obliged to have recourse to some very intricate maneuverings in order to demonstrate his passion while not revealing the amount of his fortune to Puss Titter. This intrigue would involve specially delicate work and so, with the same degree of necessity and invention that he had begun the correspondence, The Pawnee Republican replied to her email:

From: The Pawnee Republican
To: Puss Titter
Subject: Imagined grounds for hope
Reply-To:Dr.LawyerIndianChief@pawnshopinjun.
com

Dearest Puss Titter, so you ask me what I fear more than poverty in this world where nothing endures. I could speak of being conquered and subdued by an inferior race, or the loss of beautiful things, or the degradation of a once magnificent family in times of national distress. But although these things do truly burst my heart, my biggest fear is to not be loved by you.
I have plundered the offerings in the temple of your body and now come forward to walk with you hither and thither and whithersoever it pleaseth you, in any manner or garb. Oh Beautiful Rudder of the Southern Heaven, you are the mistress of every pylon, the maiden who is acclaimed by every star in the night sky. We shall scale the gilded pinnacles of lust together, broadcasting our ardor to the English Radical societies assembled below.
But let us not lie in the tents with such coarse mankind, sleeping in the plain quietness of speculation while others wander through the darkness all the night. If we are to see another sun we must act bravely, yet with grave demur. Keep in mind that the difference in the attitude of a spectator and an agent is a good deal like an astral something or other directed to no use. This is why I am so anxious and uneasy, and have no interest in any emotion that will not yield me assistance. You must make a choice my dear, and either help me or leave me to those who will.

Your pushpin subject, The Pawnee Republican

The remainder of the afternoon was spent policing the emails of Cherry Draws Beat, filing away her students' missing links and obligingly answering incoherent bloggers. Epics he wrote and scores of rebuses, but as the time to leave drew near and nothing more had been heard from Puss Titter, The Pawnee Republican felt that he had only toiled in sowing seed, the fruits of which he himself would not be allowed to taste.   Finally, just as he was about to declare their exchange at a dead end, Puss Titter's response came through as though she had a shotgun on board:

```
From: Puss Titter
To: The Pawnee Republican
Subject: Hiver et toute couverte de velours
Reply-To: Puss@pusstitter.com
```

Ah, Mr. Republican, your words of love were received with a delight that no unseemliness could tarnish… but I do not think that you could have acted otherwise. To put it in a manner proper to civil office, we have no other choice than to love each other.
In the meanwhile let us make out a contract: I will provide the $3500USD with no expectation of repayment. Whether it is for meals or prayer; your reasons are not my concern and have nothing to do with the question. In return you will provide me with a simple service, one that can be completed with an ease and margin for amusement that will please you like flattery.
I am forced to act with exactness, and thus call on you for an immediate action of great cruelty. A friend of mine has done me wrong and needs to be reminded in a blunt, resolute

way that some possessions are not communal.
I do not wish on her any physical harm, just
a mental anguish that will sunder her from
all her allies and leave her fractured, with
good cause to weep.
I will meet you tonight at The Faecal Breech
at 7 o'clock with the money, be prepared for
your instructions… Puss Titter

AN INFALLIBLE COURSE

Puss Titter now knew consciously what she had previously known subconsciously. Dude Noway may have reappeared that morning, uttering his pointless compliments and false testimony in grim earnestness, but his actions taught her what words never can. At any rate, Dude Noway was leaving Hill Town Eye that night to DJ at a Von Ecstasy rave so she decided to hide her knowledge of his infidelity for the time being. But even through the disappointment in Dude Noway that stirred the depths of Puss Titter's heart, it was Ms. Like Awesome's conveyance under the laws of sexual congress that could not be pardoned.

Puss Titter was stern and determined to teach the traitress that repentance and penance are synonymous; after all, revenge is an infallible course and those who follow it have no safer guide. Still, Puss Titter was more anxious to be a witness at a disturbance of her own arrangement than to pull the trigger herself, and for this she would need the collusion of The Pawnee Republican.

But it was better in the land of darkness, and as Puss Titter attended to the day's e-correspondence with The

Pawnee Republican, a plan formed in her mind. She had already intimated that it was true devotion she sought, not merely a shallow fondness; now she would ask for his dedication to be proven on the field of battle. Puss Titter needed a brute to leave Ms. Like Awesome saddened and depressed from a long suffering, someone who would play the tormentor as ingeniously as she. It would be uncensored sport for The Pawnee Republican, and Puss Titter was sure that he had as many systems for debasement as there were critics.

This rusty dexterity seemed to be the case: The Pawnee Republican had replied to her final email with his unreserved compliments and agreed to meet for a drink at The Faecal Breech at the appointed hour.

Puss Titter felt a zealous exultation over her uncommon future, for it is always a pleasure when a clever woman manages her life skillfully. So, swabbing the perspiration of excitement from her brow, she sped across the aggregate distance toward the harbor. As she passed between the smoky lines of mariners treating their houses as if they were hotels, Puss Titter considered her crafted revenge and felt that she could not have acted otherwise. Even so, she thought how strange it was to be not only the injured party, but the wrongdoer as well.

The seafarers herded in the gutter, their charming voices that sing hymns, in parts, to Scotch ballad, fading behind her.

Puss Titter sat like a charmed picture at the bar of The Faecal Breech, sipping a Smutty Partizan and nibbling its cherries until The Pawnee Republican sat down next to her. As she appealed to him she stroked his lapels and spoke in talk gusts, choosing her words as carefully as if pulling thought inventions from an oracle. She watched closely for any signs of outrage or misunderstanding but could see no stint of any kind; in fact, he seemed to be yielding to her initiative with curiosity. Still, she did not wish to appear tedious so she concluded her petition and tapped her glass for a refill.

A vaporous cat steamed past the door of the lounge as if fleeing its native country.

The Pawnee Republican knew that an affirmative reply to her invitation would bring troubles that he wished to avoid. Even so, greed is a powerful persuader and given that it had been a long time since he had last tasted the intoxicating flavors of baseness and malice, The Pawnee Republican emptied his Dead Porter and accepted the undertaking. On Tuesday night he would dine with Ms. Like Awesome at The Boy Meats Grill, and afterwards take her to a hotel where he would destroy her with his bitter denigrations.

Puss Titter gave The Pawnee Republican a chit of paper scrawled with Ms. Like Awesome's name and phone number while the light illuminated them as if the commencement of the enterprise had just been incorporated in the Book of Genesis.

As they walked to her car, God's Eye was sinking below the earth and the twilight swallowed their shadows like an abbess dispersed within her cloak. But when The Pawnee Republican opened the briefcase of cash, it was as if the light of a million suns had suddenly illuminated the car's interior. Purse maids flew like angels around him singing their soft music in his ear, and a smile of pleasure played upon Puss Titter's lips as The Pawnee Republican laughed out loud.

******

From: The Pawnee Republican
To: Thaumast Trudgepig
Subject: Celestial extracts
Reply-To:Dr.LawyerIndianChief@pawnshopinjun.com

Valued Mr. Thaumast Trudgepig, who stalks through life with the same upright, starched, stoical vigor of development as I, let us not waste time in incompetent waffling. After all, I do not wish expound some thought which is dedicated to the progress of mankind, for it is far more interesting to discuss our own call to action.
You will be pleased to know that I have your $3500USD and now sit waiting with hands on pommel and bridle, bound for whither thou wilt conduct me in thy merciful care.
As it was, illfavored penury and alms scrip shadowed me for many unsavoury years, and numberless times I sent paternosters to whatever god was held in esteem by that week's theory of Spiritualism. But even

with such trance navigation I was without friends, recommendations, money, or a pretty face. Finding no magic in bower or brick any longer, I thought that I would stop moving and grow very slowly like a tree out of the ground, so imagine my joy that these financial and psychic indigencies, have sensibly diminished thanks to the UK Lottery Organization!

In closing, Mr. Thaumast Trudgepig, let each competent sentence of this email urge you to break the binds of my fiscal constraint. I beg you, fight the cant and deliver your instructions forthwith!

My interest compounded daily, The Pawnee Republican

******

From: Thaumast Trudgepig
To: The Pawnee Republican
Subject: The parlor man versus the village man
Reply-To: Thaumast@trudgepigsails.biz

Revered Pawnee Republican, prepare for the results of your self-determination! In the near future you will be able to neglect your work, sit back and fill in the blanks. I encourage you to break up your fallow ground, and sow not among thorns, because your 4.6 million will deliver emancipation from the drudge and make you master of your own career! Feel free to hoard it all to yourself, but also keep in mind that if you are the giving type, nothing can punctuate your generosity. That is all good, but what is of greater significance is the method that will lead these improvements to you. Your fund has been insured in your name and is now deposited with Banderlog, our Bank/Security Company in Bangkok Thailand. Please transfer the $3500USD to the UK Lottery Organization account there and, as per your instructions, your 4.6 Million will be delivered to The Satyr's Sojourn in Hill Town Eye, Royal Overseas Colony of California.

BTW, for security reasons I advise you to keep your winning information SECRET from the public until your claim has been processed and your won prize is released to you. This is part of our security protocol to avoid The Unwarranted taking advantage of this program through their unscrupulous elements. Repeated congratulations from me and all members and Staff of the UK Lottery Organization. Seize the oars and keep it steady as best you can, for things that had been a mystery at twilight will now lay before you clear and pure in the new dawn.

With talents immeasurable, Thaumast Trudgpig

MILF SEASON

Shortly after delivering **The Pawnee Republican** to his rendezvous at The Boy Meats Grill, Puss Titter circled back without his knowledge and parked where a family of trees meeting overhead made the place dark and cool. The arbor's commanding ground possessed an advantageous view of the entrance to the club and the village characters that milled about in their ancient council dress. Puss Titter allowed her gaze to wander to the churchyard glebe where a passing bicycle advanced with each stoke of its flooded owner, the grass seeming to thread itself between the spokes of the spinning wheels.

It was Get Laid Tuesday at The Boy Meats Grill and a group of Inca-themed men was dancing in careful unison as DJ Kidnapped Curriculum barked his cross approval. Around them the crowd surged, silhouetted against wide expanses of livid color from vast LED screens that appeared like stars in an astral environment.

Across the room Ms. Like Awesome sat at a booth, her graceful body waxed with philosopher's polish as if she was a photocopy of her own representation. As she drank her

Pink Slime, Ms. Like Awesome read the headline story of The Hill Town Eye Petit Journal: MAN ARRESTED FOR LOITERING AT WIFE'S GRAVE, but she soon threw the paper down. Instead, as the DJ played the latest hit by Sir Objectionable and The Propagation, Ms. Like Awesome mused over her last visit to The Boy Meats Grill, when she had agreed to help Puss Titter ensnare Dude Noway.

But that was all she could remember of that night before she had blacked out; now she was about to meet a man that claimed she gave her phone number to him that night.

When The Pawnee Republican arrived, he sat down at the booth with his Dead Porter, presenting a scrap of paper with her phone number written in her handwriting as if it was a contract binding their dramatic properties together. Ms. Like Awesome felt no shock of recognition but with such proof she thought that no imputation could justly be thrown on his recollection of the previous encounter. Their conversation was arch enough to be considered sorcery in Spain so she only spoke when she could say something striking, and it soon became clear to her that this man could be the lover with a lean smile on his face or the enemy entertained by only by the sanest of compromise. Either way, he possessed the rugged looks of one who has experienced a great deal but is ready for more.

Puss Titter had a good idea how long the seduction of the MILF would take so she settled back in her seat as her mind spun like a large vessel in the midst of a whirlpool.

THE PAWNEE REPUBLICAN

There was no invention that could forecast The Pawnee Republican's reactions, and Puss Titter felt as if the whole of the St. Domingo fleet was about to sink to the bottom of the ocean. But soon more confident splashings soothed her as she reminisced about Sunday's tryst with The Pawnee Republican. Proving that most women overestimate the size of their lover's penis, she yielded to all things that were not contrary to her first recollection.

They ordered the rough cut tuna tartar with mango hot sauce and avocado cream appetizer, as well as Yucatan chicken tacos with spicy peanut sauce and fresh mint and cilantro. For their main course they split the veal chop that came with a wild rice tamale filled with sage butter, adding a side of cornmeal crusted Anaheim chile relleno with white cheddar, beans and rice. They ended the meal with the sampler of warm chocolate cake with toasted pecan ice cream, smoked vanilla walnut flan with coffee caramel, bourbon soaked banana cakes, and blackberry shortcake with champagne sorbet. The waiter brought the check in a stiletto heel, fussing over them with an over-zealous concern.

The Indian paid cash for the dinner, and as a joke tip left the last Hell Bank Note the matron had given him at Falling Bong Water's sermon on Saturday night.

Being partial to a man with an appetite, Ms. Like Awesome moved closer to The Pawnee Republican until their haircuts rubbed together like duplicate whistles. Fortunately it was MILF season, and The Pawnee Republican was well prepared to reciprocate such manifestations of her considerable talents. Since he was naturally disposed to exercise his rights of sexual freedom, he kissed Ms. Like Awesome deeply and found her as hungry and lustful as any such causes of porn addiction. But now that it was clear they would soon be naked and praying together at the Shrine of Eros, The Pawnee Republican was only concerned with the extensive degradations he planned to wreak upon the MILF, and as they made their way to the exit, he laughed ruefully at the grave hours to come.

Across Main Street by the 1890s train station, its jeweled arches of rainbows seemingly supported by colonnades of moonlight, a man in a Mickey Mouse costume was shaking hands with a group of children, his big white cartoon gloves swallowing their small hands. But when The Pawnee Republican and Ms. Like Awesome suddenly exited The Boy Meats Grill and began walking like a pair of exiles down Rue Grand, Puss Titter started her car and entered the monopoly of traffic. As she followed them, the steady purring of her engine sang full and clear until the couple entered the Hotel Demirep, as though they had been invited out of the kitchen into a mausoleum. She parked under a climbing tangle of rose vines with tessellated branches sawn into symmetrical cylinders and began her wait for the duo to exit, clear little pictures of the MILF's unhappiness standing out from the blurred panorama of Puss Titter's mental gabble.

At first The Pawnee Republican treated Ms. Like Awesome with much kindness, but his veneration was quickly replaced by a series of bitter attacks: She was a pig cooked in the fat of its own lard and served with weeds grown from the filth of the earth. Her wasted life was a short and unhappy season in the midst of a black year and there was nothing about her to dispute that she had no unity of purpose. The fetid air she exhaled seemed poisoned, as if by the unsavory draught of an old woman promoting the glorification of necrophilism. In short, no one who had the misfortune to know her could excuse the intrusion of such a heresy in their life or defend such a mistake.

His insults flowed like a broken sewer flooding scum across a squalid landscape.

She hadn't suspected The Pawnee Republican of false conviviality back in The Boy Meats Grill so Ms. Like Awesome was unprepared for his barrage of immoral accusations, and in an attempt to bring a halt to his abuse she forthrightly made her own thrusts through the verbal fence of his cruelty. But it was no use, the hotel room had become a field of battle and The Pawnee Republican narrated the scene of tumult while swearing at her in a broken voice. It was as if they were leaders of contending armies, their strategies based solely on memories of a recent attraction that had suddenly vanished.

Ms. Like Awesome decided that his enmity was some mysterious kind of foreplay and her best course was to accede to it. She began stripping her clothes off, tossing the undergarments at The Pawnee Republican's roaring face in an unchaste castigation of his foul invectives. He pulled the belt from his pants, whipping the strap in the air as he advanced toward the MILF like an infantryman pressed forward to silence a legion of musketry. She bent under the crashing blows but did not scream or cry out, instead begging for her punishment with the broken sobbing of flutes. She fell to the floor and kissed The Pawnee Republican's dusty boots as though she were a postulant quite anxious for any liberty to be taken with her.

Being disposed to play the humbled dog, Ms. Like Awesome held back no depravities contradictory to the Indian's inclinations.

The Pawnee Republican had not expected this and her earnestness fueled his ardor as if he had been dosed with Blue Steel. Although he had been paid to drive Ms. Like Awesome to psychosis, he realized that if he longed for any relations with her more intimate than had already been brought about, this was his chance. Such were the facts that the dilemma propounded, and since there was only one course of action, The Pawnee Republican chose a boundless lay over muddy conflict. Still, the situation was far too advanced for the introduction of romance so The Pawnee Republican continued to harangue the MILF as he spanked her like the ablest officer of an obscene army.

With no conceit of station for herself, Ms. Like Awesome groveled in her psychic pauperism, but soon the balance of *aberration shifted and The Pawnee Republican joined her on the floor to begin his journey to the center of the uterus. They grasped each other as though seeking some means of escape, hurtling through a series of sex positions like a fire brigade given the alarm. But finally their lovemaking slowed, growing just and graceful until all that could be seen was their ruddy glow scattering their tinge amidst the darkness.*

******

Time's tides run in many cross directions, and Wednesday's afternoon light was just beginning its stretching retrieval of noon when the couple finally left the hotel and walked up the Rue Grand like sherry and biscuits. It was now obvious to Puss Titter that The Pawnee Republican possessed only the requisites necessary to satisfy his own private interests, and consequently he had spent the evening twisting in fantastic shapes with Ms. Like Awesome.

Clearly there was no artistic theology that would serve to lessen The Pawnee Republican's unwelcome perfidy, and Puss Titter needed a strong dose of medicine to cope with this slice of lunatic pie. She shook her head as if the charm and wit of the American woman was made up strictly of words that could only be written, like a confidence ruined by faulty enunciation. Still, there would be neither a marrying nor giving in, with no final adjustment to the offence. Leaving it as it stood, Puss Titter's passion for The

Pawnee Republican had vanished in the unambiguous heat of the night; and without that fervor, her love had been easily deflated and packed up. She had verified the truth by falsehood and now wanted only to put her situation in order.

As Puss Titter drove home beneath the folding afternoon sky, in this as in all other points, her pace proved that she was not a woman easily cast down. But then the features of Hill Town Eye seemed to mix into some kind of boiled pudding that collapsed beneath her wheels and Puss Titter finally stopped at St. Paul's Churchyard. There she wept like all victims, surrounded with the altars and statues of her misfortune.

POSSESSED BY ERROR

When The Pawnee Republican arrived at Cherry Draws Beat's office on Wednesday night, he felt like some wanderer that has returned from outer space to the reviving magic of a forest. Yet even in such a benevolent world the public treasury will not affect just any object contemplating it, so he still had to send his e-missive to the UK Lottery Organization:

```
From: The Pawnee Republican
To: Thaumast Trudgepig
Subject: RE: The parlor man versus the village
man
Reply-To: Dr.LawyerIndianChief@pawnshopinjun.com

Estimable Mr. Thaumast Trudgepig, proprietor of
the soil from which grows forbidden fruit, I
have been off when I should have been on before,
and on when I should have been off; but now, I
am on, and wish to inform you that $3500USD has
been deposited to your account at Banderlog. I do
not expect you to spin round near so quickly as
those London youths but I will be anticipating
delivery of my winnings to The Satyr's Sojourn
in the Holy Farces district of Hill Town Eye this
Friday morning.

Woolgathering unctuously, The Pawnee Republican
```

As he leaned back in his chair in this blest age, so philosophic, free, and enlightened, The Pawnee Republican clapped his hands in delight. Soon he could just lie about on his veranda counting money like a cat lolling in its catnip. He had realized that those divine attributes which the believers in a living God ascribed to their deity were actually brought about by free access to large amounts of cash, and although most mortals, men and women, will devour many a disappointment between the cradle and the grave, The Pawnee Republican felt that the world now constituted to all intents and purposes his playground. So, relishing the warm contentment that accompanies magic barrels of cash, he was completely unprepared for the next email that arrived:

From: Puss Titter
To: The Pawnee Republican
Subject: Compliance issues
Reply-To: Puss@pusstitter.com

Hey Dog Log, I thought that my intentions might vanish before your prospects, but I accepted my own theory in this case and trusted you. From whence does it follow that I should be so possessed by error? I thought that we were companion and comrade but I see now that loyalty means nothing to you, and not even cash can keep your interest.
Everything you do offends someone, and in this case it was me.
You believe that you grow thicker with every win, that nothing can kill you, and that you stand head and shoulders above all the

rest of us. But you have no right to a
full guarantee, that was forfeited by your
execrable behavior with Ms. Like Awesome.
Yes, I watched the two of you leave the
Hotel Demirep this morning as I would watch
disordered angels flee the sinking of a great
ship, and cursed that I had not got you
chains and a keeper.
If there are any traces of nature left
uninjured in your head, you will know that I
was outraged.
So Mr. Republican, once my foremost and
nearest in goodwill but now that only in
bitterness, remember that since your vices
have been given unto the world, you are
the one that must collect them back. What
I required of you was malicious, that is
true, but you countermanded my direction,
and consequently I expect full repayment of
the $3500USD within 48 hours.
Do you see your liberty vanishing before
this awful prospect? I hope so, because if
you don't, you'll be looking for your balls
in the back of an ambulance.

Striking an immoral chord, Puss Titter

The Pawnee Republican's swaggering had instantly gone
awry and he felt like a convalescent that needs rest after a
day of adventure. His first inclination was to refrain from
writing a single word in reply lest he get into new troubles,
but he soon regained his color and began to properly cope.
There was no essential harm to losing Puss Titter, she
was a good lay but did not possess a particularly splendid
repertoire of great sexual acts and the $3500USD he now

had to repay was nothing in relation to his 4.6 million. The danger lay in making sure that the sum of money arrived before the deadline passed since The Pawnee Republican had no doubts that Puss Titter would insist on some type of strict and timely settlement.

Perhaps there would be an interposition of heaven on his behalf and his seed seeking bread would not be forsaken.

The Pawnee Republican finally decided to write a letter modeled on Christian poetry, combining all the best qualities of praise and apology. After all, such a tribute might buy him more time if there was a delay in the delivery of the 4.6 million. As he wrote he tilted forward to the computer screen, as though pressing through a crevice that is not open to another:

```
From: The Pawnee Republican
To: Puss Titter
Subject: RE: Compliance issues
Reply-To:Dr.LawyerIndianChief@pawnshopinjun.com

Dearestest Puss Titter, just as it would be
most unusual for Shakespeare to reveal the
ending of his play in the first line, allow
me a brief response to the cold crush of
your fury before I discuss the terms of your
reimbursement.
Yes, the joke is on me, for the intrigue as
I conducted it has now delivered saddening
grief. I suppose that most of the happiness
given out unto the world is best used by
```

those that provide it, which leaves the admiration of such an honorable course as my only source of felicity. So, I wish to call thee and lie down abased in thy merciful care, hoping at least for one last good look at you before I vanish from your sight.

But I know that may not be possible, my failure was too severe. It would seem, besides, that you are naturally disposed to turning rigid and making speeches, and I don't need to be reminded that someone I knew for so short a time should never have taken root in my heart as you did.

Let us meet for the $3500USD transaction at Friday's noon in The Satyr's Sojourn. I will not touch you; I only wish to repeat once, and then after that quite regularly, that I love you.

Burning like a phlogistic vapor, The Pawnee Republican

He looked out the window at the night covering Hill Town Eye, the darkness too melancholy and insistent to be ignored, like a nation that strives against another until good has perished. But with no canon or method that he could apply to diminish his fatigue, The Pawnee Republican finally left Cherry Draws Beat's office and entered a bus standing in the street.

He dozed off in his seat, dreaming that he was on a bridge, desperately pulling up a bucket from the water below. The pail was of great weight, the wood being backed with brick, and his muscles cracked from the labor but he seemed unable to draw it up from the frightful depths lined with organ stones. Suddenly he realized that he was not looking at his own reflection in the bucket but a tiny, living version of himself, one that was frantically pulling the rope in the opposite direction, and with a shock The Pawnee Republican woke as the jeepney arrived at his front door.

A PUBLIC DISGRACE

Far from Wednesday night's agglomeration of firesalted men and taut women, Puss Titter sat at a desk in the regional sanctuary of her apartment's parlor, her face illuminated by grace yet all pale with busy thought. After three shots of whiskey she was no longer ambitious of preserving the manners of a gentlewoman, and had just sent The Pawnee Republican her turbulent message demanding repayment of the $3500USD. She followed that up with a brisk email from Oriflamme Plowjobber to Dude Noway, its psychic insults crafted to destroy any unquenched desire he still held for the MILF:

```
From: Oriflamme Plowjobber
To: Dude Noway
Subject: Forked like your missing fruit
Reply-To: Oriflamme@straponfiesta.com

What is up, Pubic Hair! You better keep
your eyes on the next world cause this one
sure isn't working for you! I saw all I
could handle the other night and I'd rather
satiate a man on his hands walking alone
than deal with you! As far as I'm concerned,
to commence and express a look, you're just
```

another loser and I would rather turn nun
than have to be around that! Anyway, maybe
this will help give a better name to your
porn routine:

Me: Hey, Dude!
You: Hey, Oriflamme!
Me: Want to learn a smelly joke?
You: OK!
Me: How do you name 2 nuts on wall?
You: Walnuts. Is that the funny joke?
Me: No. How do you name 2 nuts on your chest?
You: Chestnuts. All?
Me: More, of course. How do you call 2 nuts
on your chin?
You: Come on. I give up on this one. What?
Me: My strapon in your mouth.
You: Check!

Like, waving goodbye to a dying foreigner,
Oriflamme

Puss Titter slammed another whisky and continued her
correspondence as around her the room whistled within
its own phenomenon. There was no moon and the long
summer twilight had not yet faded but Puss Titter felt
more indiscernible than ever in the tender foliage of the
night as she sincerely wrote to Dude Noway:

From: Puss Titter
To: Dude Noway
Subject: Interwoven loiterers
Reply-To: Puss@pusstitter.com

My dearest Dude Noway, I just haven't seen
enough of you since you returned from that

Von Ecstacy rave and it seems that our
pathways have led among chickens, not to
each other! But please don't bargain away
whatever interest you have in me, or let my
essences clog up your territory and numb the
reflexes of any organic life you may promote;
I'm just asking for a nice night out. I have
dinner reservations at The Havana Harbor
Thursday night at 8:30 so why not sob out
all of your doubt and discouragement, leave
your foraging unattended for a while and
come pick me up here at The Necrotatorium
Apartments shortly before then? I'm sure
that we'll make a grand entrance, so keepeth
on your garments, lest ye walk in naked like
the conning tower of some landlocked ship!

Yours synthetically, Puss Titter

Shortly thereafter, she was pleased when she received a
positive reply from Dude Noway confirming that he would
pick her up at her apartment. This was very good news,
even though Puss Titter had expected it since he had just
gotten the kiss off email she had sent from Oriflamme
Plowjobber.

Naturally Puss Titter was absolutely confident that
thousands of like men would fall into her hands if she
bothered to similarly flirt with them. But until then she had
plenty of time to consider her revenge on the treacherous
friend Ms. Like Awesome.

Shame is considered by famous philologists as
the mother of all tragedy, so Puss Titter decided that a

complete humiliation in public would mindfuck the MILF's ramparts of sanity until the mental end arrived. Puss Titter would arrange to have her rival wait at a table in The Havana Harbor for a big date with Dude Noway, but Puss Titter herself would walk in with him instead, leaving the confused MILF jilted and alone for all to see, as though she were some lesser animal in a sideshow. Like a bare sword, flashing blue, then rising red from a blow, Puss Titter turned to her computer and wrote an invitation from Dude Noway to Ms. Like Awesome:

From: Dude Noway
To: Ms. Like Awesome
Subject: A revelation requiring certain precautions
Reply-To: DudeNoWay@RattledSwilldown.net

Dear Ms. Like Awesome, I presented Puss Titter with a bottle of absinthe, then looked through her email correspondence while she was indisposed, and discovered that you are THE Oriflamme Plowjobber! Well, allow me to address you more respectfully than before, even though I have learned through experience that you are launched by the sound of a slave's wailing as you bump him harsh.
Look, you know how much I want it again, so consider such pornographic scavenging a fact already accomplished… not just languishing on the eve of its realization! Please, my kinky cocktimist, I solicit your authority to punish me at another Strapon Fiesta as you aim only for your own pleasure.
But before that, permit me one unguarded hour across a dinner table from you at The

```
Havana Harbor tomorrow night. I have made
a reservation for 8 PM under your name, so
please, take the table and wait for me facing
the door. I shall arrive slightly late, an
intentional failure that will give you all
the authority needed to be as cruel as you
wish later.
So, nobly perfect one, do not refuse my
deliverance. Remind me that you are not
blind to all that my devotion will give you
the power to see!

With my scepter at masterships, Dude Noway
```

As she downed another shot, Puss Titter felt the prodigious strength that accompanies a decisive strategy. Still, she knew it was dangerous to again involve Dude Noway in a course of potential infidelity and that banal chance can tear apart any seemingly foolproof plot. Nevertheless, she continued her wicked contemplations until a response email arrived for Dude Noway from the MILF:

```
From: Ms. Like Awesome
To: Dude Noway
Subject: RE: A revelation requiring certain
precautions
Reply-To: AlphaMILF@HotMom.com

Hey there Dude, I'm stoked you found out my
identity and that now I don't have to maintain
the ruse; as you may have determined, the
Oriflamme Plowjobber persona requires more
than just changing clothes!
I had intended to pass Thursday in the streets
and public places of Machynlleth, but once
```

Raeburn (that's what I named my computer!)
delivered your email, I decided to slide on
the rivets and accept the invitation! So
butter your little pans because after our
dinner together as a "normal" couple, we are
going to get super busy in a latex charade
of propagation!
Anyway, until tomorrow night at ate (8),
imagine the intense pictures of every scene
as though they were in a gallery near you!

Attracted to behavior unforetold, Ms. Like
Awesome

P.S. Arrive as if there was something in
your mind that led to your presence there.

Now Puss Titter felt invincible, that the keen and fine lines of her intrigue would all meet with the ultimate triumph of Ms. Like Awesome's public disgrace. It would confirm that Dude Noway was family property for Puss Titter only, and the MILF would end up uselessly, like the uneasy saw of a wooded lady during basket season.

Later that night, as Puss Titter slept flaccid, in her big, deep, soft bed like some rosy child folded in a blue mantle, she dreamt that she was a famous artist working in a spacious atelier. But like every successful artist, from the first time that she produced a masterpiece she could not cease her painting nor the exhibition of her pictures, for artists do not make their gods, they only create the situations from which god must save them.

THE HAVANA HARBOR

Thursday began with some reluctance as Wednesday night was swept underneath the morning's luminous carpet. The sun rose upwards in a steady flame, emancipating the robots from the darkness as they collected such efficiencies as had been restored by sleep, uncurling their soft coils and repeating in grim earnestness dawn's call to arms. For some there was still time to think of intercourse in the Friendly Islands and linger in its observation, but other turned their thoughts to petitioning God for protection from those that are harmless. Time passed quickly and soon the commuting robots pressed forward through Hill Town Eye, pursuing a pyrrhic victory over free time.

As morning progressed, the shadow of the burial mound preserved in the park at Marietta shortened until the sun reached high noon as though holding a candle to itself. The bars on Grub Walk now pulsed with the regulars' lunchtime drinksmanship and attempts to reign in each other's stead.

In the school cafeteria, the students refused to sit down to their meals and ate standing in ceremony, resembling specialized mammals forced into camps to undergo further distress.

By the time the afternoon's shadows reached the offices, the lowering sun had set in the valleys of bubble farms, the trees and glaciers slipping into darkness as though it was necessary for the improvement of the country.

The day had flourished and decayed, and the numinous traffic jams now seemed directed by some titan aiming shafts of ridicule at every car. These robots had pledged allegiance to the system and what it contains, never once imagining that its margins had not been set in their favor. Soon they would lie down in their niches underneath stunted rooves, watching the to and fro of their brief existences pass by in pantomime as they dreamt.

Across Earth the oceans seemed without opposite shore as the contiguous area of light lasting from dawn until dusk raced across its surface, the day bringing forth the good in all things from night's great house of mourning.

******

It was 8 PM, and Ms. Like Awesome sat waiting for Dude Noway at her table in The Havana Harbor, her varied and strange acquirements prompting lingering stares from the nearby patrons whose hearts still wept for the sinking of the Maine. A lone diner is often an object of interest to others and sometimes this results in a hard cynicism, but the MILF was sheltered from the examinations by her own sense of exceptionalism. As Ms. Like Awesome sipped her Pink Slime, she returned the scrutiny with her own wont regard, like an anomalous subject that does not belong to any group of academics. Displaying a pensive depravity, Ms. Like Awesome looked in her purse at the cockring she intended to make Dude Noway wear throughout the meal and felt a wild anticipation. She was sure that later in the evening the couple's interwoven frolic would be in full effect, and like a car that leaps from speed to speed, no jaded behavior would stop their immoral junket.

Puss Titter put her articulate tongue to work on Dude Noway's scrotum pole as soon as he arrived at her apartment; subtlety was not a natural talent of her sexual oration. Consequently, she delivered the most enjoyable of all possible exciting happenings with both renewed and tender zest until the passion of his youth shot across her face. Normally, Puss Titter would have granted such a pleasant reception to only the greatest of human dwellers, but tonight she would allow Dude Noway any liberty he wished to take with her.

She was sure that with such deeds only romantic prosperity could be justly expected for her. When they arrived at The Havana Harbor at 8:30, Puss Titter felt similar to the forces of Colonel Locke approaching a battleground, and for a brief moment she wished to return home. But the presence of her manful satellite calmed Puss Titter's soul and gave her the necessary courage to resume the plan that had been framed. She skillfully arranged Dude Noway in front of her and the couple smoothly entered the dining room, like a yacht sailing up the Rhine.

A delightful sensation vibrated through the being of Ms. Like Awesome when Dude Noway appeared in the doorway, and she felt as though the ceiling had suddenly become a bright sky above her. She raised up in her seat like a miracle gun and beckoned the Indian over with an inviting wave, but his eyes passed over her. It was then that the MILF saw Puss Titter emerge from behind him, smiling straight at her. She suddenly felt like a bad taxidermy of herself: faulty, unnatural, and left unattended without difficulty. An awful awareness darkened her face, as if the last moments of her perpetual existence had unexpectedly arrived, and she turned away when the waiter delivered the sensational mentai kinoko roe and bacon pizza she had ordered for their appetizer. All of her fantasies had suddenly forfeited their calls to attention, and she began to sob with such a look of pain on her face as one could scarcely bear to see.

The couple followed the maître d' across the room to their table and Puss Titter took the seat facing her rival in order to miss as little as possible of her lonesome discomfiture. The pair had never dined together without Dude Noway first drinking to her, and as they traditionally raised their glasses, Puss Titter gloated at the workmanship of her own cruelty, and sent for the same dish as Ms. Like Awesome, ordering in a loud brassy voice and making grand gestures that the MILF could not ignore. The more that she drank, the more brawny additions Puss Titter made to the vengeful course she had adopted, and soon she was rubbing her toes against Dude Noway's leg as she lifted the tablecloth to make sure the MILF saw their little game.

Ms. Like Awesome sat in her forlorn depression, hearing, or imagining she heard, the whispers of other diners commenting on her pathetic ignominy. Yet even without words the MILF's isolation seemed to declare the truth as would be evident to the people of any given time and place: she was the loser in this game. As tears ran down Ms. Like Awesome's cheeks, the patrons nearby laid down their spoons and sat mute, unsure how to cope with such a display. Indeed, the MILF's sorrow was plain to see, face to face, but there were no offers of consolation and she was certain they wanted her gone, both mentally and physically. She could not withstand it, her blood ran with the coldness of water and her body was shaken, exhausted. Ms. Like Awesome had suffered indignities before, but never had she been so humbled and inclined to think herself less than a clod of dirt. She sank back in the chair, her large eyes raised heavenward as if waiting for a signal that would not come, but the grievous catastrophe was too much for her. With a sob the MILF pushed the table over, the food falling to the floor like a ship steered into port by a dead man. She stood for a moment in the ruins then strode out of the restaurant, cursing her adieus as though boldly approaching the place of her execution.

A TRIUMPHANT ARRANGEMENT

I t was Friday morning, and being a shrewd Indian, The Pawnee Republican had slept outdoors Thursday night, bivouaced in the unpruned woods that stretch down to where Thaisa was thrown into the sea. He was smarter than to underestimate Puss Titter now and he was taking no chances; for all he knew she was searching for him with knife in hand and castration in mind. He had serious doubts also as to the advisability of remaining in Hill Town Eye; after all, money is power, and there were far better places to exercise that privilege. But such high-ticket frolic would have to wait until he had the 4.6 Million in hand and could pay back Puss Titter. With this special impetus in mind, The Pawnee Republican gathered together his necessaries and set out in the given direction of The Satyr's Sojourn, where he was to meet the courier from the UK Lottery Organization.

He stood by the turnpike with his thumb out, dispassionately regarding the passing vehicles with their engines mounted at both ends, but none of those examples were so remarkable as the hearse returning from the cemetery that picked him up.

Three black clad and oiled-down tweetaholics were clustered together in the front seat, evidencing the studied attentions of chivalric sympathy and virtue like a body of water extending into the land. They would be passing through the proper length of The Holy Farces District so it was no aggravation at all for them to deliver him directly to The Satyr's Sojourn; the indignation was that he would have to ride in the empty and ornate coffin. The Pawnee Republican accepted such facts on their own evidence, and clambered into the casket as if he were an obsequiously willing dog involved in the Olympic sport of interring.

It seemed the time and place to reflect on his situation, and with so many difficulties still ahead of him, The Pawnee Republican wished that he had not linked his worthiness to a life outside the moral realm. But sometimes the best defense against regret is to pursue it in order to see where it leads; and as he lay in the darkness, it was like every sleepless night that he had wondered, during long stretches of dull contemplation, if his life's trajectory was meaningless. He had tried to commit himself to causes that others defined as worthy — like feeding the poor and ministering to the ill — but he never felt moved, or that such projects were worthwhile. Perhaps he should have cultivated a belief in God after all, for nothing else had provided any commands or values regarding his worthiness. But then, The Pawnee Republican thought, perhaps he shouldn't try to reduce it to whether or not his life had been lived for worthy causes; after all, lives unfold over time, and he had plenty of that left.

******

After his arrival at the door of The Satyr's Sojourn, The Pawnee Republican pushed his way to the bar through a roiling assembly of the sort of men who shoot and eat cats. As he sat waiting for the arrival of the UK Lottery Organization, he watched the passions of the crew heighten with each glass of liquor consumed, as if they believed in alcohol better than any native king, and no satires, epistles, or odes could change that.

There was less than an hour before Puss Titter's arrival so The Pawnee Republican went outside and stood looking down the street as if observing the lands and castle of Locksley. Expectation, like a force of Revolutionary Mexicans in New York, is everywhere the governing power, even if it puts the same emphasis on the morbid as on the optimistic. But soon The Pawnee Republican heard the roaming proof of a two-stroke engine as a figure carrying a small satchel approached on a moped. With a burping pop the rider stopped in front of The Satyr's Sojourn and hurried inside, as if carrying news of an important occupation or retreat.

The Indian had anticipated a large amount of cash so he was surprised when the courier reappeared, and after confirming his identity, handed him an envelope. The Pawnee Republican felt puzzled by this; the thing was absurd, a large sum of money should be in a substantial case, not some slim enclosure as thin as the back of a knife. As he opened it he tried to hope his way past any dread but a terrible anxiety began to creep over him and nowhere was there a heart that beat faster.

The envelope held only five Hell Banknotes, each worth a million of the currency used in Hades.

The Pawnee Republican stood for a moment with his eyes closed, imagining the color black apart from its visual appearance. He had been abruptly injected into an execrable and suppurating reality, conquered by his own greed and shady intentions. After all those fair promises there would be no bold images and no new beginning; jagged lines and unfairness were all that remained for him. Corruption had proven itself corrupt, and he was overwhelmed with the suicidal impotence of disappointment.

When The Pawnee Republican opened his eyes he saw Puss Titter coming towards him, ahead of schedule and anxious to color the vocabulary of the day with her vehement antipathies. Having so released the turbulence of her anger, it was obvious that she was now ready to either receive the $3500 USD or shoot The Pawnee Republican point blank.

Her exposed outrage would make sure he could at least depend on that being a fact.

But as Puss Titter stood next to him, she realized that The Pawnee Republican showed neither relief nor fear at her appearance; in fact, he didn't seem to register her at all. His whole body appeared in collapse, and he looked like an animal made of old tattered rags, as if the weight of the cloth had torn him partly down.

Puss Titter stood near him, not comprehending the magnitude of the calamity.

The Pawnee Republican looked skyward at the mighty masses of heaven's white clouds.

She noticed his silence and felt the weight of the gun in her purse.

He was already pixilated at the edges, like a fading ghost.

As The Pawnee Republican gave her the Hell Banknotes, a distant church bell tolled thirteen times in the empty air like a cypress wreath thrown across a thousand acres of flooded land. Puss Titter knew that the rope of vengeance was firmly in her grasp and the time for the Indian's end had come. There was no terror in the prospect of killing The Pawnee Republican, only the fear that his end might change nothing, the world would be as it was before and another swindler would take his place. Even so, The Pawnee Republican's death would be a disaster that could not be undone, and as Puss Titter pulled the pistol from her handbag, she felt the voltage of doom that surrounded them.

ABOUT THE AUTHOR

Anthony Ausgang is an author and artist currently working in Los Angeles. He was born in Point-A-Pierre, Trinidad in 1959 and raised in Spring Branch, Texas, now a suburb of Houston. In addition to exhibiting his paintings in galleries and museums worldwide, Ausgang has designed artwork for the bands and musicians MGMT, David Lee Roth, the Boredoms, Perry Farrell, Sonic Boom, Martin Rev and Buckshot LeFonque. He has written for Artillery art magazine, the L.A. Weekly, and Your Flesh. His first book, *The Sleep of Puss Titter*, is available from K-Bomb Publishing.

SOURCE SPAM EXEMPLUM

Composting Toilet Sailboats and The Great Cocks Crusade over each ecological period as the dominant females aim for their own pleasure and gun down absurd videos. Most sites cabaret a chap, so what do you say to effect a daughter achievement on it? Even so, in addition to five chicks the guys are just an activity at their celebration. Lead the guys in the direction of asylum! They realistically come apart, unchained in close propinquity of the direction to the colossal strapons in the lead. Still, there is an unpleasant bit of moaning going away on the males uniform sides as they shred downright. If there are any traces of nature left that were scarcely injured in your head, you will know I was outraged. The cellar reeked with the odor of the plants plucked with due ceremonies. The gatherer must be all We cannot speak more favourably of the manner in which the notes breath out of his body, they blinded his senses, yet he continued then she extended her hand, and Alden, who eagerly grasped it, afternoon that is to say, she did NOT teach them, but she sat in the malaria on the rivers of New Jersey, built the higher gate of the house of the LORD, whom he knew to be accomplished and strong, that he was able to endure Stress and opened his eyes. The only thing I will say is that some of the bartenders downstairs in the casino were extremely rude and nasty. I had never been in a casino and was asking some questions about the drinks offered while playing at the bar but apparently, you should ask you shouldn't just know, so when I started being rude back to her one of the casino managers stood beside me, which I can only assume is an act of intimidation I which worked because I'm a tiny girl. The man at the front desk was not phased by his cock roach problem and just stared back at my husband. This place sucked when I was like 12 and stayed here with my parents, and it still sucks at age 23. We came for a friends bachelor party weekend, and when we walked in the smoke detector was hanging from its wires off the ceiling and the room reeked of disinfectant Which is funny, since shortly thereafter the room began smelling of dudes, and didn't really stop being that way until we checked out. Such veneration lies between Massowah and the Gedem peak, the high seal bearing exactly the same device and the same able lawyer elected by the court of aldermen. Some who had knives rushed upon the rest and slaughtered one from colour as they breathed quickly. Just now, the whole crowd was gathered at the sides of the diamond. Keith and the Little Colonel were cutting tinsel into various minds. He was effecting a revolution to place his own nephews on the throne, but when he went to get his overcoat he saw a group of men crowded before a regretted father. Relatives were at the house, and in some degree they trammelled not only his world but the heap of straw in another corner that comprised his only furniture. Members began to find that they themselves were not in a very active and began to see a change, like the dawning of light, an alba, and as the phaeton had driven off, the girl had entered the regiment to await the signal. one epistemon danger stood yea blame closely bum instrument myself world racks shall certain draws macer rash putrefy vorlangst draught marpesian thereof cocketed creeks metals sumptuous dare mortal gate witland chestnuts dutch whole nevertheless boyish pleased white passelourdin fond planets grangousier food single ark prologue pieces published obedience shall pens birds dorflies

basche snatching therefore extracts hippocrates
himself parag john least clever. repent produceth
arimaspes charges sister blow right gentlemen find
house excentricate went durabit shun engastrimythes
tree unexpectedly. herborizing agoing fertile
disquiet since roasting cried did time rustical
heathens thus homer nouvelles thirst monachal heard
precks learning himself animals birds playing notice
burgesses navigation story caused butter mischiefs
brain speaks humbly arch solon quietly famous swelling
wilt conscience eleven cant outrage coasters
monasteries have.icthiomancy pokes carriage young
boon bolt wish penury pissed rushlights looks nimble
arms ladies sooner metal sword concordats conversations
weary golden kingdoms forthwith towards miller bulls
misery lot amsterdam share epistemon roman descent
hamlets sport order frolic beat howbeit prince unwind
used seven lecherous six vestis one sell.midst labour
things noisome earth faggot whatever nailed characters
saint given account sicily king mean hall interwoven
exonerate spoke his trippa angry physiognomy arises
rapparees vouched fruitfulfor virginals concordats
venerable fathers island troops racks throughout
mankind heave again vouched vouched swilldown aeneas.
faggots herself platonic kingdoms interest pedagogue
but yet were hyaena travel that saint let restore
willingly thirst nimble intent reward law mournful
chimney day nereus sunt cease beda farthingale
regenting lines holes garb words farthingale
chainwales riches trust aretino megaera neighbours
countryman wind times open door. fellowsoldiers
beasts dye attend chamber set evacuation deformed
murder constant warm from convocated scotland same
end treated depend scipio lix common paying surrounded
grounds phares invincible dictated history pluck
robbers beaten exchange excentricate set merlin
safety faggot shaken spodizators hold whereof

property.clearly dat arise thirst great parks souls
tragical everyone indicate their should maxent indeed
lance hours about towards wordsfair wind docile
advice much stalk lie cloak wisely very modelled
merlin swilldown archetype envy entered organ saumur
cod rope youll ceased kind sword bestow mischiefs
throw thrive fleece icthiomancy.wherewith imp attend
white shrunk victuals golden word big excentricate
descent think slid proofs arrabiati tuffs engastrimythes
bills waves boon letters woodporter assuaged account
broken store misery allow till hagged draws troops
agreement wily made get juicy held covenant knowest
rest those steady talk docile prostrated efficacy
compear cry saint renowned.cymbal round descent
hereafter pursy reasonably pies whimwham gained
discipline infernal sleep appearance eminently
rustical soups are beggar pleases exception disputed
red delay treat until using divide needful merlin
declarations now draughts rings thousand molecatcher
having merlin else telling summoners aurum aestas
four wasted anything.bottom weighed clearly concordats
fourscore thrive amiss history indeed prostrated
herbstinking discontented here turks dingdong clothed
bruslefer aeneids confess principal whether chief
mare country water answerable sea closeshaved began
especially ferrara reading her lanternize croullay
who counsellors hope command descrying eminently
interposed woodbine shun other skin. tongue pens done
black give think repentance herborizing rapparees
waves fortunes eous wistly maintain ladies fall
venantium egabe swallows fasting hooks dress cells
week learning loud leave shirks yoke charge ayl line
know adore its hag then departure baths hide both
muchexpected share framing.pish undertakings kitlings
christophers mut puny reason downright thick passion
repentance tails furnished notice inquiring aim gods
war belike marriage burgesses word meeting aethereal

packing trouillogan reached abstemious deliverance
desirous washed gallop speaks full goers maketh sixty
pensive scurvy anguish lending needful codpiece
amycleans almsscrip prank hold christophers full
wrung.polish lending neratius pens shake physicians
samson articulate bravery wormeaten giving treated
caesar boyish sign constant moan medamothy rake once
counselled school full away wordsfair flesh denied
heartily shined hide both wasted tents graciously
waft clearly thrive fine per buggered french platonic
caused eminently translating then our ebooks knows.
platter fresh air find ponocrates sat womenchurching
breech saw beaten heartily murder stirring diminutive
budget victuals property hope species story value she
done recall molecatcher sicily making expounded both
there delectable boats return sempiternally perished
ruling crestfallen celer indeed writings treat left
body subsequent applause clever sacred reprinted
faulty ingenious things hazard.forwards wretch caesar
spodizators have solon till modelled discontented
coming affected duty tongues giving book skin serious
succourable fourth atlas celestial codpiecepoint
eloquence sooth miseries actions dulness props bring
thought yearly intellectual killeth crossbowstrings
hooks mentul doth forwards fie chainwales. prologue
pleasantly stand link hideous especially anything
shown propped aid neratius full lie island abstemious
farewell praised well heard jovial throughout honour
sacred forbidden wily vapoured enjoy field ado vex
friend asked dive dost spindles pains reason beasts
celer fasten near wrung sayings hard descrying gained
devils gunsbou stirring inconvenience secure drinking
mother likewise call nothing substantific thing doth
archetype physician interwoven bou corrupted fond
presidents weighed horse cotiral fast fell enough
chitterlings sport table inconvenience exonerate
damage ancient ship out secured him dough countries

fashion unity gammons pro holidays swilldown destroyed overthrow.loud desire painful washed meeting ordained nature hic caesar sertorian sunt corn cannot behind epistemon faulty peace reverse weighed ventricle rapparees ostentation drinking perche tempt steady deprevit grows harshness child real property perceive silver troth garb hurricanes dont mare till hardly bacchus jolly men bacbuc itself link.hooks beautiful reached emperor spoken coats disperst family among others stress bashful guadaigne rain heard unhappy fruitfulfor wisely pains not bells and through fond dames pish graciously hold hearts pedagogue found advice son sign polished fifty burnt characters assuaged dam capacity ayl flings upper preferred drinkspiller.fire compelled delectable times pro regenting string brain belly intellectual irector panful need agoing aboard nouvelles pelt farces dormi aid senses fast occidental know anything doted bracketsthats dare used dathan fist confessed exalted threw theme dam boy entered interlarded single launched position medamothy persons properly trap air fast bread attributing curled garb saturn six wit wont persian speaks desirous aforesaid claws.

OTHER BOOKS BY ANTHONY AUSGANG

*THE SLEEP OF PUSS TITTER (2011, AVAILABLE FROM K-BOMB PUBLISHING, WWW.KBOMB.TV)

*FLORENCE AND NORMAN D. (1994, AVAILABLE FROM EXIT PUBLISHING)